GRAVEYARD SCHOOL

1

Don't Eat the Mystery Meat!

Tom B. Stone

Toronto · · · uckland

RL 3.6, 008-012

DON'T EAT THE MYSTERY MEAT!
A Skylark Book / September 1994

Skylark Books is a registered trademark of Bantam Books,
a division of Bantam Doubleday Dell Publishing Group, Inc.
Registered in U.S. Patent and Trademark Office and elsewhere.

Graveyard School™ is a registered trademark of
Bantam Doubleday Dell Publishing Group, Inc.

ISBN 0-553-48223-8

Published simultaneously in the United States and Canada

Bantam Books are published by Bantam Books, a division of Bantam
Doubleday Dell Publishing Group, Inc. Its trademark, consisting of the
words "Bantam Books" and the portrayal of a rooster, is Registered
in U.S. Patent and Trademark Office and in other countries. Marca
Registrada. Bantam Books, 1540 Broadway, New York, New York
10036.

PRINTED IN THE UNITED STATES OF AMERICA

OPM   0 9 8 7 6 5 4 3 2 1

Trapped in the lunchroom . . .

It was pitch-black. Edging forward, Park banged into a shelf. He grabbed the edge of it and groped his way along it until he reached the door.

The door was locked. He couldn't get it open. He was trapped in the dark in the refrigerator in the lunchroom of Graveyard School.

I will not panic, I will not panic, Park told himself.

He flung himself against the door and began to scream. He screamed and screamed.

Nothing helped. No one came.

At last, exhausted, Park turned and pressed his back against the door. *I won't starve,* he thought. *And I can't freeze to death. What else could happen?*

I get caught. I get suspended for life. My parents kill me.

It could be worse.

Standing up in the darkness, Park began to jog in place to try to keep warm. It sort of worked, but he felt stupid. No wonder his parents hated jogging.

He was bounding up and down so hard that he didn't even hear the door handle turn. He had his back to the door when it opened, framing him in the dim light of the kitchen.

Other Skylark Books you won't want to miss!

GRAVEYARD SCHOOL

1

Don't Eat the Mystery Meat!

CHAPTER
1

"Attention, students. Attention!" Dr. Morthouse, principal of Grove Elementary School, raised her hands.

The noise in the auditorium grew louder.

The principal smiled. When she did, something silver flashed in her mouth.

"It's a fang," said Park Addams to Stacey Carter, who was sitting next to him. "You know it's a fang, don't you?"

"Don't be silly," Stacey answered crossly. "It's just a filling." She folded her arms and looked around the auditorium. Rows of first-graders sat near the front, twitching and peering over the backs of their seats at the other kids. The second-graders sat behind them, doing the exact same things, but ignoring the first-graders. Behind them sat the third-, fourth-, fifth-, and, in the back rows, sixth-graders, where Stacey and Park were sitting.

Stacey scowled. The first day of school. Who made the summers so short and the school years so long? Just the day before, she'd been Stacey Carter, part-time dog walker, cat-and-goldfish feeder, and plant waterer. Making money looking after the pets and plants of people who were away on vacation. Spending her free time at the community-center swimming pool with her friends or hanging out in the park with her dog, Morris. Spending her extra money at the mall.

And now this. No pay. No free time. And no respect.

She sighed and picked at the ragged edges of the hole in the knee of her jeans. Then she put her feet, in her new sneakers, up on the back of the chair in front of her.

Out of nowhere a teacher's voice boomed, "Stacey Carter, take your feet off the back of the chair."

Stacey sighed again and lowered her feet with a noisy thump.

Beside her, Park laughed.

Stacey didn't blame him. She knew Park's mood was just as evil as hers. He wasn't any happier than Stacey about being in school. He never had been. Even in first grade, when Stacey still thought it was cool to have things like reading hours and quiet time, Park preferred being outside. If he was outside playing baseball, that was even better. And baseball-wise, it had been the perfect summer for Park: He'd gotten to play with an older group of kids. He'd finally gotten good enough.

Now school was cutting into his practice time.

Principal Morthouse turned her head from left to right, keeping the smile fixed on her face. Silver glinted from her mouth as she surveyed the room.

"A fang!" said Park. "See?"

Stacey didn't bother to answer.

"Attention!" Dr. Morthouse bellowed. She grabbed the microphone and leaned over. "ATTENTION."

The microphone made a horrible screaming sound, like a dying rabbit.

Silence fell.

"Gooood," said the principal, smiling even more. "Welcome back to Grove School, students! I know you've all had a wonderful summer and are refreshed and ready to get back to work learning new and exciting things."

"Yuck," said Park. "Hey, Stace, want some seafood?"

Stacey turned, and Park opened his mouth wide, showing her the remains of a candy bar he'd been eating.

"Hold it," said Stacey. She leaned over. "Peanuts . . . chocolate . . . and something white. Euuuw, Park! I think there were maggots in the candy bar!"

Park hastily closed his mouth and swallowed as Stacey went off into gales of smothered laughter. "Gotcha!"

"Ha, ha," said Park.

" . . . and of course I expect our new sixth-graders to set an example . . . " Dr. Morthouse droned on.

"That's us," said Stacey.

Park slid down in his seat and folded his long legs so he could prop his knees against the back of the seat in front of him. "Not me. I *hate* school. And Graveyard School is the worst."

"At least we have our own graveyard." Stacey nodded toward the windows. Outside behind Grove School,

3

across the playground edged with a jarringly white picket fence, the weathered stones of an old graveyard marched unevenly up an overgrown slope. Green moss and gray lichen and the strange cold wind that never quite stopped blowing there had erased most of the words on the stones. Broken bits of pottery vases showed that people had, once upon a time long, long ago, visited the grave-yard to leave flowers. But no one ever got buried there anymore. And the living never visited the dead.

Park didn't even look in the direction of the graveyard. He rolled his eyes. "Big deal. Nothing ever happens around here. Nothing ever changes. Nothing, nada . . . *ouch*. What d'ja do that for?"

Stacey elbowed him again. "Listen," she hissed.

" . . . some very good news for you boys and girls."

Park groaned. "Boys and girls??"

"I'll let your assistant principal, Mr. Hannibal Lucre, tell you all about it, since he's the one who arranged it."

Mr. Lucre bounded forward, rubbing his fat hands to-gether and licking his lips. He brushed back the long strand of hair that he kept combed over the bald spot on the top of his head.

"Good news!" he cried.

Mr. Lucre was almost as universally despised as Dr. Morthouse was feared. The noise in the auditorium be-gan to build again, but Mr. Lucre's next words put a stop to it.

"I know you will all be sorry to hear that Mr. Todd, the

4

lunchroom superintendent for Grove School, has retired."

A small cheer broke out in the back. It quickly died down when Dr. Morthouse turned her silver smile in the direction of the noise.

"All *right,*" muttered Park. "Decent."

"And I am pleased to report that we have a new lunchroom superintendent. She's an excellent cook who has studied in *Paris.* Without further ado, let's all give a warm welcome to Ms. Gladys Stoker!"

As a tall, thin, ghostly pale woman marched to the microphone, Dr. Morthouse and Mr. Lucre began to applaud loudly. They were the only ones.

Ms. Gladys Stoker didn't seem to notice the unenthusiastic reception. She inclined her head regally, as if to a cheering crowd, and held up her hands. Dr. Morthouse and Mr. Lucre stopped clapping.

"Thank you," said Ms. Stoker. She had a gravelly voice that went up at the end of each sentence. "Thank you all. I'm delighted with this challenging new job. This year, I can promise you, we will take new directions in nutrition and flavor. We will take your tastebuds where they have never been before. You will be served rare delicacies, special treats. Together we are going to revitalize your vitamins and pump up your protein!"

"What a Froot Loop," said Stacey.

"Shhh," said Park.

"And all," Ms. Stoker's voice went up and up in excitement, "ALL . . . while keeping the cost low, low, low. Lower than it has ever been before! This is my promise to you."

She threw her arms wide, lowered her eyes modestly, and stepped back as Dr. Morthouse and Mr. Lucre applauded more wildly than ever.

"I wonder which spaceship *she* comes to work on," Park cracked.

Stacey kept staring at the unholy three standing on the stage at the front of the auditorium: Fang Morthouse, oozy Hannibal Lucre, and the definitively odd and exceedingly skinny Gladys Stoker, a woman who apparently never touched her own cooking.

"You know what?" Stacey whispered to Park at last. "I've got a bad feeling about this. A really *bad* feeling."

The lunchroom line moved slowly.

"What's the holdup?" Jaws Bennett complained. "I'm hungry."

Perfect Polly Hannah pursed her lips disapprovingly. "You're always hungry."

Jaws looked sadly down at loose pants he was wearing, barely held up by a tightly cinched belt. "It's true. I never get anything except sprouts and tofu burgers at home, now that my parents have started eating health food."

"Sprouts are *extremely* high in nutritional value," said Polly. "Plus tofu is the best protein you can get without eating meat."

6

"Hey, Jaws," said Park, giving him a shove. "I thought you'd eat *anything*."

"I used to think so too," said Jaws.

"Well, we're going to get some real meat today," said Stacey. "Look."

They'd reached the front of the line. Above them on the wall hung a big sign with the words: SPECIAL FOR THE DAY—MEAT LOAF SURPRISE IN MASHED POTATO CRUST.

"Lemme at it," cried Jaws joyfully, grabbing a tray.

"But didn't you bring your lunch?" asked Polly. She pointed to the bag in Jaws's hand. "Are you going to *waste* good food?"

"Oh, yeah. Right. Here, Polly, you take it." Jaws shoved the bag onto Polly's tray and rushed forward through the line. His pale-blue eyes gleamed with anticipation.

Polly looked in the bag and recoiled slightly. "What is this?"

Slamming two servings of meat loaf special onto his tray, Jaws looked back. "Leftover carrot-lentil loaf with pureed spinach sauce on forty-grain bread with high-protein spread."

"It's slimy and green!" wailed Polly.

"Don't waste food, Polly," Park chortled as he pushed by her and followed Jaws down the line.

"Boys are so gross," said Polly, coming up to the table where Stacey was sitting with Maria Medina. Polly

7

put down her tray and adjusted her pink headband in her carefully arranged blond hair. She smoothed her new pink-and-yellow-flowered shirt, carefully tucking it into the new matching yellow skirt she was wearing. She checked her tights to make sure they weren't wrinkling at the ankle. She checked her new pink flats to make sure no scuffs had marred them. Then she sat down.

Maria caught Stacey's eye. She and Stacey were both wearing jeans, like most of the kids in their class. Stacey was wearing a sweatshirt with a blown-up photograph of her dog, Morris, on the front. Maria was wearing a giant rugby shirt. Maria's dark bangs stood up in spikes from her habit of running her hand through them. Stacey's long brown hair was pulled back in a braid. She'd started wearing it that way over the summer because she thought it made her look more responsible to her clients—the human clients, not their pets.

Stacey and Maria had never even seen Polly in jeans. It didn't look like she would be wearing them in sixth grade, either.

Stacey shrugged. Over at the table where Park was sitting, she could see that the guys were playing seafood again.

Looking down, she studied her plate. The broccoli looked sort of like a small tree, but it was a bright neon green color. Mashed potatoes oozed out from around the Meat Loaf Surprise. Stacey picked up her fork and gave the meat loaf a tentative poke.

Was it her imagination, or did the meat loaf move?

"What exactly is meat loaf anyway?" Stacey asked.

"Meat," said Maria. "And, ah, other stuff."

"Like what other stuff? Have you ever thought about that?"

"You mean, what kind of meat? Hamburger." Maria tasted the meat loaf and made a face. "I think. This tastes kind of funny. Like when it's my big brother's turn to make dinner."

"Maybe that's why she calls it special. The lunchroom super, I mean," Stacey said, giving her meat loaf another poke and watching it closely.

Polly had cut her meat loaf into sections and was chewing each one efficiently. "What do you mean, it tastes funny, Maria? It tastes just like last year's food."

"That's because it is last year's food!" Stacey laughed loudly. She was the only one who laughed at her joke.

Polly kept eating, being careful not to get anything on her new flowered shirt.

Jaws shouted from the other end of the table, "This is great! From now on, I'm saving my allowance for lunch."

"No." Maria shook her head seriously. "I mean it. The meat loaf tastes weird."

"Lunchroom food always tastes weird," said Stacey. She speared the meat loaf, held it down, sawed off a piece, and ate it.

"See?" said Maria, watching Stacey. Maria took another tiny bite. "Ugh. I wonder what's in it?"

"It's just meat loaf," said Polly. "My mother always puts oatmeal in hers. And onion soup mix. You know, things like that."

"Oatmeal?" Maria's expression said that she didn't think oatmeal was much of an improvement. She switched her attention to the neon green broccoli. She cut a small bite and ate that. "Hey, this isn't too bad."

"Broccoli! You like the broccoli better?" asked Stacey.

"Yeah," said Maria sheepishly. "I do."

Stacey chopped off a tiny piece of broccoli and put it in her mouth. "You're right. It does tastes better."

"Broccoli is a nutritionally sound choice for many important vitamins," intoned Polly. "Are you going to waste your meat loaf, Stacey? Maria?"

"Do you want it?" asked Stacey. "Here."

"Take mine too," said Maria.

Polly frowned. "I don't know if I can eat all that."

"You could put it in a doggie bag," suggested Maria, "and take it home to your dog."

Polly frowned harder. "No, I can't and besides, he's not my dog, he's my mother's."

"Why not?" asked Stacey. "I mean, why can't you take a doggie bag home?"

"Because Sweetie Pie is missing," said Polly. "She went out yesterday morning to . . . you know . . . and never came back. My mother is very upset."

"If my dog, Morris, disappeared, I'd go *crazy*," said Stacey, staring at Polly. "Aren't you worried?"

"Why should I be? She isn't *my* dog, she's my mother's. My mother was always kissing her and talking stupid baby talk to her." For a moment Polly's normal expression of smug superiority was replaced by a look of anger, but it quickly disappeared. She added, "Besides, Sweetie Pie was messy."

"I bet she just got lost," said Maria. "Have you called the Humane Shelter?"

Polly shook her head. "No. Sweetie Pie would never, *ever* wander off."

"That's 'cause she's too fat," Park added as he sat down next to Jaws.

"Sweetie Pie had big bones," said Polly calmly. "She wasn't fat."

"You should call the Humane Shelter, Polly," Stacey urged.

"My mother has already," said Polly. The idea didn't seem to please her. She put her fork down.

Jaws said, "Are you going to eat all that meat loaf, Polly?"

"No, I guess not," said Polly regretfully. "You may have it." She pushed her plate over to Jaws.

He grabbed a fork and took a big bite.

His eyes widened. He opened his mouth.

"Gross!" shrieked Polly. "Stop that, Jaws! Stop that this instant!"

Jaws opened his mouth wider. His eyes bulged out. His face turned bright red. Bits of meat fell from his mouth.

"Jaws! Jaws!" cried Park.

Jaws gasped. He clutched his throat. Then he fell to the floor of the lunchroom like a dead man.

CHAPTER

2

"He's dying!" screamed Maria.

"He's dead, he's dead!" shouted Park.

Polly leaped up from the table. "Stop it!" she shrieked. "Stop it this instant!"

Jaws's head fell to one side and his tongue lolled out.

Putting her hand over her mouth, Polly began to turn a sickly shade of green.

"Jaws? Jaws?" Park knelt down beside him.

Jaws didn't move.

"Gross," whimpered Polly.

Park grabbed Jaws by the shoulder. "Jaws? Jaws, speak to me!"

Students at other tables jumped to their feet to see what was happening. Chairs scraped. Voices rose. In no time at all a small crowd had gathered around the limp figure on the floor.

"Dial nine-one-one!" someone called.

"Do mouth-to-mouth resuscitation," said someone else.

"Does anyone know the Heimlich maneuver? Who's had first aid?" asked Maria, looking around. "You have, haven't you, Stacey?"

A murmur went through the students who were watching. Stacey didn't like the sound of it one bit. She looked around. Where were the teachers when you needed them? she thought. Oh, sure, a pop quiz, and they were right there, red pencils ready. But when it came to something important . . .

"Stacey!" said Maria.

Reluctantly Stacey knelt down beside Jaws. She lifted his limp, unwieldy body up and propped it against her. She looked around. Still no teachers. With an inward sigh she put her arms around Jaws from behind and prepared to do the Heimlich maneuver. Balling her hands into fists in the center of his upper abdomen just beneath his ribs the way she'd been taught, she squeezed Jaws with all her might.

Jaws's eyes popped open. He flopped back against Stacey and stared up at her, a maniacal grin on his face. "Gotcha!" he shouted, and began to chew rapidly.

"Ahhhh!" Polly shrieked. She jerked backward and crashed into a group of boys.

"Polly's got a boyfriend, Polly's got a boyfriend," chanted Jaws, still chewing at top speed.

With a mighty shove Stacey pushed Jaws away and jumped to her feet. "You are a world-class jerk!"

14

"Good one, Jaws," said Park, giving Park the Spock Vulcan sign from the old Star Trek reruns.

"*What* is the meaning of this?" said another voice.

The crowd vanished.

Getting to his feet so fast, he looked like he was levitating, Jaws gulped and choked. Quickly Park began to pound Jaws on the back.

"Something he ate, Dr. Morthouse," Park told the principal. "That's all."

Dr. Morthouse didn't say anything. Jaws managed an unconvincing cough. Finally Dr. Morthouse said in a steely voice, "Do you need to see the school nurse, Alexander?"

When no one answered, Dr. Morthouse frowned. "Alexander?"

"He means you, Jaws," said Stacey.

"Oh. Right. Uh, no. No, I'm just fine now, thank you, Dr. Morthouse." Jaws swallowed noisily. "See? All clear."

Raising one eyebrow, Dr. Morthouse said, "Very well, then."

She turned and strode out of the lunchroom.

"Ha, that *was* a good one, wasn't it?" said Park, giving Jaws a punch on the shoulder when Dr. Morthouse was out of earshot.

"Just great," said Maria angrily. "Just great! Next time you need help, don't ask me, Jaws. I don't care what happens to you!" She picked up her tray and marched angrily away.

"What could happen to *me*?" asked Jaws, grinning. "Hey! Maria! Hey, you said I could have your meat loaf! I hadn't finished!"

"You're disgusting," said Polly, turning her nose up in the air and walking off in the other direction.

Park and Jaws looked at Stacey expectantly.

"Not bad," said Stacey. "I *almost* believed you. But just remember the story of the boy who cried wolf. Like, suppose you called for help and nobody came?"

"Nah. I repeat, what could happen to me?" said Jaws triumphantly. He sat down at the table and pulled Polly's tray toward him. Park sat down too.

Stacey looked down at the lunch congealing on her plate. "What *could* happen to you, Jaws?" she asked thoughtfully. "It's a good question. I'll give it some thought."

With his fork halfway to his mouth Jaws stopped. "Your meat loaf," he suggested. "Your meat loaf could happen to me. . . . "

Stacey shoved her tray toward Jaws. "That'll have to do for now. But you're going to get it, Jaws."

"Gee, thanks, Stace," said Jaws.

Shaking her head, Stacey left Jaws and Park. Her heart was still pounding from Jaws's dumb trick. For a moment she'd believed him. She'd actually believed Jaws against all her best judgment. When she'd known Jaws was faking, she'd let the crowd of people, all staring at her accusingly, pressure her into actually kneeling on the floor and . . .

She stopped herself from thinking about the scene. *Dinosaurs will make a comeback before I ever fall for one of Park's or Jaws's stupid jokes again*, she told herself.

At least I didn't scream, she thought. *Park would never let me hear the end of* that.

"How did you like it?" said a gravelly voice.

For a moment Stacey thought she was being asked about the stupid fakeout that Jaws and Park had just pulled. She made a face. Then she realized who was speaking to her: Ms. Gladys Stoker, new lunchroom superintendent for Graveyard School. In the skinny flesh.

And she was talking, Stacey realized, about lunch. Hastily Stacey arranged her face into a teacher-appropriate neutral expression.

But she couldn't help staring. Ms. Stoker in the flesh was just as strange as Ms. Stoker at the other end of the school auditorium. Maybe even stranger.

Oh well, thought Stacey. At least the new lunchroom super had actually asked about lunch. No one else ever had.

Aloud she said, "The, er, Meat Loaf Surprise? Oh. Well, it all got eaten." That at least was the truth. Or would be in just a few minutes, at the rate she'd left Jaws chowing down.

Ms. Stoker didn't seem to notice Stacey's evasion.

"Good, good, *good,*" she said. She reached out and tapped the long, thin fingers of one hand against the top of a box attached to the wall next to her. "I want input. I *welcome* input."

"That's nice," said Stacey, watching Ms. Stoker's fingers go up and down, up and down.

"My little suggestion box," Ms. Stoker explained. "So that you can write in and tell me how you feel. I'm very interested in how you feel." Ms. Stoker reached toward Stacey with her other hand, two fingers poised like a vise, as if she were about to take a pinch of Stacey's arm. But at the last minute she seemed to think better of it. She drew back. "*Very* interested," she repeated.

Tearing her gaze from Ms. Stoker's thin white fingers dancing like chickenbones on top of the suggestion box, Stacey heard herself saying, "That's great, Ms. Stoker. You know what? *I'm* very interested in the meat loaf."

The fingers stopped. "Really?" purred Ms. Stoker.

"I'd love to have the recipe. Both my parents like to cook and . . ."

Ms. Stoker's eyes moved suddenly behind the thick lenses of her glasses, like startled fish in an opaque glass bowl. "How delightful!" she said, and began to laugh. "But didn't you see the sign? Meat Loaf Surprise! If I told you what was in it, what would be the surprise?"

What's so funny? thought Stacey. *Adults are such psychos.* But she smiled politely and waited for Ms. Stoker to finish enjoying the joke.

Whatever it was.

Ms. Stoker stopped laughing abruptly. Her eyes flashed again as she focused on Stacey. "I noticed you were enjoying your lunch with friends. It's so nice to have friends. Very important to adapt socially. The boy in the baggy green pants—is he a good friend of yours?"

"*Jaws?* No way! Jaws is *Park's* friend, not mine. I mean, I've known Jaws since first grade and everything, but, well, I guess Maria Medina and Park are more my good friends."

"Jaws. What an odd name."

"It's Alexander, really. But no one ever calls him that except, you know, Dr. Morthouse and Mr. Lucre and his parents. Jaws'll eat anything. Even roadkill." Stacey laughed.

Ms. Stoker didn't. "Roadkill?" she repeated. "Interesting."

Stacey stopped laughing.

Staring across the lunchroom at the table where Jaws and Park were sitting, Ms. Stoker went on, "But—is he sick? He looks like he could use a good meal. Poor boy."

"Sick? You bet he is." Stacey tried out another laugh on the lunchroom super.

Ms. Stoker's eyes went fishy again behind her glasses, and Stacey cut herself off mid-laugh to say hastily, "I mean, no, he's not really sick. That was just a joke."

"Ah. Very interesting . . . and it's a fashion, to wear his pants so loose?"

"Jaws doesn't care about fashion. What happened is, his parents went on this health food diet and he's lost all this weight. On tofu and bean sprouts and things like that."

"Tofu?" Ms. Stoker's narrow nostrils flared. She shuddered. "*Tofu?* Poor, poor, poor boy! His pants, his shirt, they used to fit? Yes, he looks like he used to be so nice and—*healthy*."

"He liked your lunch a lot," Stacey volunteered. "Maybe he'll gain some weight back from your cooking."

This time Stacey wasn't trying to be funny. But Ms. Stoker started to laugh. Her eyes narrowed into slits. Her thin lips slid back over her big teeth. "Ha, ha, ha," she cried. "Ha, ha, hahaha." She was still laughing as she turned away from Stacey and walked jerkily back into the lunchroom like a big windup toy.

"Ms. Stoker? About that meat loaf?" Stacey called after her.

But even though she'd stopped laughing, Ms. Stoker didn't seem to hear Stacey. Stacey thought she heard the lunchroom superintendent mutter as she walked out of sight, "Interesting. Verrrry interesting."

The first day of school was finally over.

Stacey and Park were riding their bikes home along Grove Road. Graveyard School was out on the edge of town, and the road wound past farmhouses and fields before it reached the street leading to their neighborhood.

One day down, thought Stacey. *About two hundred to go.*

Well, maybe not two hundred. But it would feel like two hundred.

"This is where I turn," said Park, jerking Stacey out of her thoughts.

Stacey looked up. "You're not going home?"

"Baseball game," said Park, waving his hands in the direction of the baseball fields in the Grove Memorial Park.

"Maybe I'll see you over there later," said Stacey. "When I take Morris for his walk."

"Morris," said Park thoughtfully.

"My dog. Morris. Remember?" said Stacey sarcastically.

Park ignored her. His eyes were on the distant baseball fields, still an inviting green in the golden fall sunlight. School was over for the day. He'd already forgotten about it. His baseball glove was in his backpack and he had more important things to do.

Except for one thing. His eyes narrowed. "You know what I think?" he asked.

"Think? You? That's a good one," said Stacey.

"I think Polly had something to do with her mother's dog disappearing. That's what I think."

Stacey laughed. "Yeah, right. Polly probably wouldn't even let that dog near her. She hated that dog."

But Park wasn't listening. The crack of a bat against a ball was pulling him like a magnet.

"See ya," he said, and pedaled off, his eyes fixed on the baseball field.

Stacey shook her head. She tried to imagine Polly stealing her own mother's dog—and doing what with it? Polly couldn't give that dog away. No one would want it. Early in the summer Stacey had walked Sweetie Pie once. Just once.

And told Mrs. Hannah, politely, that she couldn't do it again. She'd said her schedule was full.

Mrs. Hannah, a larger, pinker, frillier version of Polly, had cuddled the nasty little dog with the pop eyes in her arms and said, "Poor ittle sweetums. No walk-walks? Boo-hoo."

Stacey had made a hasty exit. She didn't want to stick around and explain that Sweetie Pie was the meanest, nastiest, most foul-breathed rodent of a dog she'd ever met.

Plus he'd wet her foot when she wasn't looking.

She didn't think Mrs. Hannah would have listened.

Stacey wondered how Polly felt about her mother's blind devotion to the evil ittle sweetums.

Hmmm.

Maybe Park wasn't so far from right after all.

CHAPTER
3

It was Saturday at last.

"The first week of school is always the longest," said Maria.

"I think the last week is the longest, when you're waiting for it to end," said Stacey. She looked down at her dog, Morris, who was walking facefirst into the new piles of fallen leaves. "Dogs are sooo lucky. They just hang out and sleep and eat and chase squirrels and bark."

She and Maria were on their way into the park. The first week of school had just ended.

Morris turned right and pulled Stacey over to the community bulletin board by the park entrance. He put his nose down and sniffed furiously.

"Wow, listen to this: 'Toilet for sale. Good condition.' " Maria made a face.

" 'Parrot missing,' " Stacey read aloud. " 'Reward.' "

Maria grinned. "Maybe the first grade should put a sign

up about the missing ant farm . . . euwww: 'Iguana lost.' I hope it's not lost around here!"

Morris snorted. Stacey laughed. "Would you like an iguana, Morris? I bet you would."

She let Morris lead her and Maria into the park. He snuffled and made funny gargling sounds in his throat as he strained forward. Morris loved the park. It was full of wonderful things to smell, like old sneakers and garbage cans. And wonderful things to eat, too, although Stacey never let him eat the really good stuff, like mashed squirrels and dead pigeons.

Pulling the two girls, Morris made his way to his favorite bench and flopped down by it. The broad swath of meadow in front of them was empty in the late-afternoon light, but they didn't have to wait long before a man walked up the path from the other side, calling over his shoulder, "Spot! Here, Spot! Here, girl!"

Maria rolled her eyes and said, "Nobody calls their dog Spot. Not in real life, anyway."

A dalmatian bounded out of the bushes in the park with an enormous stick in its mouth.

Morris went on stick alert, leaping to the end of his leash. His skinny white tail slashed the air furiously. His little black eyes gleamed in anticipation.

Spot's owner clapped his hands. "Gooooood girl. Good girl. Come here, girl."

Joyously Spot circled her owner, holding the stick just out of reach. The man laughed and reached for the stick. Spot leaped away.

Morris made a choking noise and pulled harder on his leash.

"Calm down," Stacey told Morris. She raised her voice. "Can he play?" she called to the man with the dalmatian. "Can my dog come and play with yours?"

The man looked up. "Sure! Maybe they'll wear each other out."

Unhooking Morris's leash, Stacey said, "All right, Morris. Go on."

Morris launched himself like a missile at the dalmatian.

"I can't watch," said Maria, putting her hands over her eyes. She looked through her fingers and started to laugh as Morris seized one end of the dalmatian's stick. The two dogs began to drag each other back and forth over the grass.

"Dogs are so funny," said Maria.

"They're pretty weird," agreed Stacey.

A bike screeched to a halt behind the bench. "Hey! Are you guys talking about my sister, Susie?"

Stacey and Maria knew who it was without turning around.

"Hi, Park," said Stacey.

"Hi, Park," said Maria.

"How weird is my sister?" Park said as he propped his bike against the back of the bench. He walked around to join Maria and Stacey. "She's so weird that the aliens beamed her back down." Park was always making fun of his older sister.

"I thought she *was* an alien," Maria answered.

Abruptly Park lost interest in the joke. "Yeah," he said. "Hey! Did you see all the signs on the bulletin board?"

"Like what?" asked Stacey.

"Like all those animals are missing?"

"People always put lost-and-found notices on the park bulletin board," said Maria, her eyes on Morris and Spot.

"There are signs up all over town. Dogs. Cats. Boa constrictors. Hamsters."

"Hamsters?" That got Maria's attention. "Hamsters are running away from home now?"

"How do you know there are signs all over town?" asked Stacey.

"I get around, that's all," said Park.

"Any missing animals in your dog-walking business this summer?" he asked Stacey.

"No!" said Stacey indignantly. "I'm very responsible!"

"Sorry," said Park. He waited, but neither of the girls asked him any more questions. Finally he asked, "Wanna play some catch?"

"What happened to the baseball game?" asked Stacey.

"We won," said Park. "You wanna play catch or not?"

"Sure," Stacey answered. "But neither of us have gloves with us."

"I have an extra one. We can take turns."

"Okay . . . Maria, you go first while I keep an eye on Morris."

Out in the middle of the park Morris had gotten the stick and was running in circles at top speed to keep it away from Spot.

Removing a rubber band from the collection she kept around one wrist, Maria pulled her dark hair back with it. Then she put the glove on and thumped her fist into it. "Start slow," she ordered Park. "I don't want to pull any muscles or anything."

Soon the ball was going back and forth between the two with a rhythmic thump, thump, thump. It was a soothing sound.

"My sister," said Park, "is on another diet."

"What kind of diet?" asked Maria.

"I don't know. Something from one of those dumb magazines. When I left this afternoon, she was eating a grapefruit. I *hate* grapefruit."

Stacey looked at Park over her shoulder. "Park! I thought you'd eat anything."

"That's Jaws, not me," answered Park, refusing to let Stacey get to him. Maria wound up and burned a ball into Park's glove.

The smack made Park yelp. "Hey! Gimme some warning next time!"

"Here's your dog." Stacey turned back around. Spot the dalmatian and her owner were standing there. The man was holding a black leash fastened to Spot's black-and-white plaid collar in one hand. His other hand was on Morris's purple collar.

"Oh!" Stacey was surprised. "Thanks. But you didn't have to do that. Morris never wanders off in the park."

As if he understood her, Morris flopped down at Stacey's feet, panting hard.

The man shook his head. "You can't be too careful." He looked around, then lowered his voice. "Dognappers."

"Did you say dognappers?" asked Park. He moved closer to the bench, giving Stacey a triumphant look. Maria moved closer too.

"That's right. Dognappers. Right here in our town."

"Tell me more," urged Park.

"How do you know?" Maria asked the man. "About the dognappers?"

"Two dogs have disappeared off my street this past week," said the man. "Vanished. Just like that."

"That's awful," said Stacey sincerely. "But maybe they just wandered off. I mean, Morris has gotten out before at home, and every time he has, we've found him hanging out with a bunch of other dogs. You know, dogs are pack animals and they like to do things together, like—"

The man shook his head emphatically. "No. These dogs disappeared on different days."

"Some stupid people just let their dogs run around." Maria made a face. "Then the dogs get lost or the pound gets them."

Again the man shook his head. "These dogs belonged to responsible owners," he said. "They were both in fenced-in backyards. *And* the gates of both yards were closed. And locked."

"No holes dug under the fence, no other places they could have gotten out?" asked Park.

"No."

"No ransom notes?"

"No, but a very big reward has been posted for one of the dogs. Although personally, he was not a *nice* dog, if you know what I mean. Spoiled. Overfed. Bit people. And other dogs." The man lowered his hand to the top of Spot's head and stroked it gently.

"Was the dog named Sweetie Pie?" asked Park.

The man looked surprised. "How did you know?"

"I'm a sort of detective," Park explained modestly.

"Well, you shouldn't blame the dog for being spoiled and mean," interrupted Stacey. "That's not the dog's fault."

The man thought for a moment, then said, "I suppose you're right. Well, gotta go. Remember what I said now. Be careful with that dog of yours."

"Hear that, Morris?" asked Stacey. She reached down and fastened Morris's leash to his collar.

"Wait a minute, wait a minute, I've got an idea!" Forgetting that he still had his glove on, Park raised his hand to his forehead and gave himself an unexpectedly hard whack. He staggered backward, then straightened up. "Maybe Polly didn't off her mother's dog!"

"Duh," said Stacey.

Maria looked puzzled.

"Dognappers," cried Park. "It really was dognappers, like the guy said!"

Stacey was about to make another sarcastic remark, but stopped herself as Park explained how he'd first thought Polly had gotten rid of Sweetie Pie. "A crime of passion, see?" he explained. "But now I realize it must be a ring of professional dog thieves."

It was remotely possible, Stacey supposed. Quickly she reached down and checked Morris's leash to make sure it was on securely.

"Wouldn't that be *great*," Park was saying. "Dognappers! So I solve the case, get the reward, we find Polly's mother's dog, who Polly obviously doesn't like, *and* Polly's mother pays us this big reward. Polly's gonna *hate* that."

"So you're gonna catch these dognappers," said Maria. She snorted.

"Forget it, Park, you couldn't even catch cold!" added Stacey, tugging on the edge of her bicycle shorts. The two girls burst out laughing.

"Are you laughing at me?" demanded Park, his face getting red.

"I'm not laughing with you," said Maria.

"Go ahead and laugh, then. But when I'm counting all the reward money, don't come to me for any interest-free loans!"

"Yeah, yeah, yeah," said Stacey. She stood up. "I should go, I guess. It's getting kinda late."

"Yeah. No way I'd be in the park after dark." Maria

took off the glove and handed it to Park, who stuffed it in his backpack.

Stacey shrugged. "We've got Morris."

"Morris is a cream puff. A cupcake. A doggie marsh-mallow. Aren't you, Morris?" Park rubbed Morris's head and ears, and Morris wagged his tail furiously. The four of them began to walk slowly out of the park through the long, late-afternoon shadows.

"You think there really are dognappers around?" asked Maria.

"Of course," said Park.

"Well, if I lived with Polly Hannah, I'd run away from home," said Maria.

"Now *there's* a motive for becoming a missing dog," agreed Stacey. "Admit it, Park. Sweetie Pie left home because he couldn't take Polly anymore."

Park shook his head. "After I finish gathering the evidence, you'll be sorry you laughed!"

As they walked between the two enormous stone lions that stood guard on either side of the entrance to the park, they didn't hear the bushes rustling. Nor did they notice the shadowy form crouched there or the beady eyes peering out, watching until Maria and Park and Stacey and Morris disappeared from sight.

CHAPTER
4

Park stopped dead. Stacey crashed into him. "Hey!" she complained.

"Do you see that?" Park said, his voice dropping to a dramatic whisper.

Stacey saw. It was the menu board by the door of the lunchroom, announcing the day's menu. Today it read CANNIBAL STEW WITH CARROT FINGERS AND POTATO EYES.

"Ha, ha," she said sourly. The day before, it had been Turtle Soup. The joke had been the small, turtle-shaped noodles swimming in the odd concoction. Each day the names got weirder, and the food tasted worse.

Why hadn't anybody else noticed?

Mr. Lucre lurched by just then, rubbing his hands in anticipation.

"Mr. Lucre," said Stacey, grabbing the assistant principal's sleeve.

Mr. Lucre turned, a look of impatience across his moon-round face.

"Mr. Lucre, what exactly does that mean?" Stacey pointed at the chalkboard.

Following the direction of Stacey's finger, Mr. Lucre let out a bray of laughter. "Oh, excellent, *excellent,*" he cried, and rubbed his hands together even more vigorously. "What a sense of humor! What an original way to tempt young appetites!"

"Cannibal Stew doesn't exactly tempt *my* appetite," said Stacey. "I mean, what's in it?"

Still studying the chalkboard and chuckling, Mr. Lucre said, "It's beef stew, of course. You youngsters are so squeamish! You must get over this squeamishness if you expect to do well in life! Look at me! I admit, I was a squeamish young man once, but I put it aside in the name of a higher calling! Educating young minds! Civilizing young persons! And, with the aid of outstanding artists such as Ms. Stoker, nourishing young bodies as well."

Stacey's mouth dropped open.

Standing behind Mr. Lucre, Park made a "crazy as a bat" motion with his finger, circling the air by his ear with his forefinger.

Mr. Lucre turned, and Park instantly began to scratch his head.

With surprising swiftness in one so chubby, Mr. Lucre grabbed Park's arm and then Stacey's. Before either Park or Stacey could say anything, he was escorting them into the lunchroom. "Come, come, come," he said. "We

34

don't want to hurt our new lunchroom superintendent's feelings, do we? Let's be members of the clean-plate club, shall we?"

He escorted them to the end of the line and left them there with a big smile. "Happy eating!"

"The clean-plate club?" muttered Park as they went through the lunch line. "I'd like to clean his plate!"

"Shhh. He's still looking this way," Stacey warned.

The two watched unhappily as their plates were heaped with Cannibal Stew. *At least,* thought Stacey, *it doesn't smell too bad.*

"Could I have an extra roll, please?" she asked at the end of the line. The cafeteria worker shook her head. "Sorry," she said. "We're all out. Seems like everybody's asking for extra rolls lately."

With a sigh Stacey followed Park across the Caf. Today Jaws, Maria, and Polly were all sitting at the same table, along with skateboarding fanatics Skate McGraw and Vickie Wheilson.

No one seemed to be eating much except Jaws. As Park and Stacey sat down, Skate and Vickie got up.

"Not members of the clean-plate club, are we?" Park sang out in a Mr. Lucre voice.

Skate rolled his eyes and Vickie made a horrible face as the two carried their trays over to the garbage.

"Polly, what are you doing?" asked Stacey.

Polly was cutting her Cannibal Stew into tiny square pieces on her plate. "It saves chewing," she said.

"You haven't even started eating," Maria said. She was eating her roll, her stew untouched.

Looking over her shoulder, Stacey noticed to her relief that Mr. Lucre had wandered off, perhaps in search of Ms. Stoker. She spooned up a bite of Cannibal Stew, sniffed it, and plopped the spoon back in the bowl.

"The bread's not bad," said Maria.

Polly kept on cutting her food into smaller and smaller pieces.

"That's all you ever do anymore," said Park to Polly. "Cut your food into tiny little pieces. You never eat it."

Polly didn't answer, but her eyes moved furtively from side to side.

"Do you have a guilty conscience about something, Polly? Is that why you're not eating?" Park asked.

Clearly, thought Stacey, he hadn't given up on the idea that Polly had offed her mother's dog. Maybe he even thought she was kidnapping all the other dogs as a cover. Ha, ha.

"No!" said Polly. She picked up a bit of carrot and swallowed it. "See?"

"I do the same thing when I don't want to eat something," Stacey said. "Cut it up into little pieces. That way it looks like I ate some of it anyway."

Polly put her knife and fork down with a clatter. "Excuse me," she said, and stood up, picking up her tray.

"Polly?" said Jaws plaintively from the end of the table.

Polly looked down at her tray, then back at Jaws. It

seemed for a moment as if she was about to cry. Then she took the roll off her plate and shoved the tray toward Jaws.

"*Bon appétit,*" she practically snarled, and walked away.

"Hunger," said Jaws wisely. "I can understand that. It does strange things to a person's brain."

"If some people only had a brain," cracked Park.

Maria sighed. She'd finished her roll. "We're all hungry these days. Doesn't anyone realize how truly awful this food has gotten? Maybe we could talk to the principal. I mean, if Polly's not eating . . . "

"Forget it. They all think Ms. Stoker is wonderful. Especially Mr. Lucre." Briefly Stacey told Maria and Jaws about their close encounter of the weirdest kind with the assistant principal at the door of the lunchroom.

"The suggestion box," said Maria, beginning to sound a little desperate.

"Yeah, *right.*" Park, who'd been eating his stew slowly, shook his head. "If you sign any suggestions, you're in trouble. And if you don't sign it, they won't take it seriously. Suggestion boxes are always a plot to weed out troublemakers."

"Well, I'm going to write an anonymous note and say that this food *stinks,*" said Maria stubbornly. "How can you eat it, Park?"

"I've had worse," Park said. He nodded in Jaws's direction. "Jaws's parents are health food freaks, but my sister is a diet donut. Like her brain has a hole through the middle when it comes to food. And every time she goes on one of her stupid diets, she offers to cook. And every time she cooks . . . " Park made an expressive and very realistic gagging noise.

Swallowing hard, Stacey said, "Knock it off, Park. The question is, what are we going to do? At this rate we're going to starve to death."

"I'm not," said Park. But Stacey noticed that he'd only eaten half his stew before putting the spoon down. Carrot fingers and potato chunks and gristly bits of meat swam in the gray stew broth like the flotsam and jetsam from a sunken ship.

"You will," Stacey predicted. She jerked a thumb in Jaws's direction. "He's the only one that's not suffering."

They all looked down the table at Jaws. Jaws looked back, his mouth working at top speed, his face cheerful. The hollows under his cheeks were filling out. His pants weren't as baggy as they used to be. In fact his clothes were not loose at all anymore.

Sighing, Stacey shoved her tray toward Jaws. "Here," she said. "I give up."

"Me too," said Maria, following suit.

Jaws's eyes brightened. He chewed ferociously and swallowed with a gulp. "Thanks, guys," he managed to get out, before shoving another big spoonful of stew in his mouth. "You know, you ought to give Ms. Stoker a chance. She's always pretty nice to me when she talks to me. Asks me if I'm getting enough to eat and every-

thing. She even asked me what my favorite food was."
Jaws took another big bite. "And I've gotta tell her, this
is it."

Park watched Jaws gobble up the Cannibal Stew for a
moment longer, then gave up, too, and pushed his tray
down the table. He looked around at the others.

"I'm afraid we're going to have to do it," he said sadly.

"No!" cried Maria. "We can't! We're in sixth grade!
Sixth-graders at Graveyard School do *not* do that!"

In a defeated voice Stacey said, "Maria. What choice
do we have?"

Maria leaped to her feet and clasped her hands together. "No!" she declared in ringing tones. "No, no,
no! Never. I'd rather die first!"

CHAPTER
5

Maria stood for a long moment, staring in horror at Stacey and Park. Around them the noise of the lunchroom was as loud as it had ever been. Maybe louder.

Hunger was turning the students into animals.

And breaking their spirits.

When neither Park nor Stacey answered, Maria slid slowly back into her seat.

"You can't mean it," she whispered. "That's for babies. First-graders. And people whose parents . . . " she nodded in Jaws's direction. "No one voluntarily. I mean, no sixth-grader here at *our* school . . . "

Again no one answered. The three sat silently as the war-zone noise of the lunchroom raged around them and Jaws continued to chew.

At last Stacey said, in a strangled voice, "I'm afraid we have to, Maria. But if we do it all together, it won't be so bad. And think about it! We'll be able to eat lunch again."

"I'll do it," said Park. "Even if it kills me."

At last Maria nodded. "Okay," she said brokenly. "Okay. I'll . . . " she bowed her head, then lifted it bravely. "I'll bring my lunch. Tomorrow. But no lunch boxes, understand?"

"Brown paper bag," said Stacey soothingly. "And don't forget to avoid using plastic. It's bad for the environment."

Park snorted. "How can you talk about the environment at a time like this?"

That night Stacey lay awake staring at the ceiling while Morris snored on her feet. She'd worked so hard and long to make it into sixth grade. She'd enjoyed taking her lunch when she was a kid, but it was an unwritten rule at Graveyard School: No one after fourth grade took their lunch—unless, like Jaws, their parents forced them to. It was the only forgivable deviation.

But now it had come to this. Turning over, Stacey thumped her pillow hard. It wasn't fair. In the morning she'd have to get up and endure the curiosity of her father while she fixed her lunch, the casual insults of her older brother. Fortunately her mother slept late, and her baby sister was still just a baby.

But she still flinched at the thought of the day ahead. As she dropped off to sleep, she made a vow: Somehow, someway she was going to get even with Gladys Stoker for this.

• • •

Maria slipped furtively down the dark hall. Her family was asleep. But determination had kept her awake until the clock had struck midnight.

Carefully, cautiously she slipped into the kitchen. She turned on the light in the pantry and cracked the door so that she could see what she was doing as she opened drawers and cupboards. Working as quickly and quietly as she could, she assembled lunch: a peanut butter and jelly sandwich, an orange, and three chocolate chip cookies. She made a face as she shoved the food into the plain brown bag and took it back up to her room with her. Not that she didn't like all those things, but it was a kid's lunch. At least for now, however, her family didn't have to know—especially her little sister, who looked up to her. It was going to be tough enduring the sneers of the other students when they saw her eating her homemade lunch. But it was going to be worse shattering her little sister's illusions about her sophisticated older sister.

"Did you have a nice time at the park with your friends?" asked Park's mother at dinner.

Park shrugged. "It was okay. We won our game. I saw Stacey and Maria afterward. Stacey's dog found another dog to play with. Then the dog's owner started telling us all about these dognappings that are happening, see?"

Park's father said, "You know, it's been a few weeks now, but it does seem to be more than just a couple of lost dogs . . ."

Susie, Park's sister, looked at Park and laughed meanly. "And you're going to solve the mystery, just like Nancy Drew. Isn't that smart of you, Park."

Park shot his sister a nasty look, then looked down at his dinner plate and groaned. "What is this? Don't I have enough to endure without coming home to a dinner that looks like dog food?"

"Park, your sister worked very hard on dinner. Mind your manners," said his mother.

"You haven't even tried it," added Park's father, picking up a forkful. "It's . . . it's . . . it's different."

Park hid a smile as his sister said, "It's Beef Stroganoff made with nonfat yogurt instead of sour cream."

"You know," said Park, pushing the Stroganoff to one side as best he could and concentrating on the rice clumped underneath. "My life is turning into a twisted Hansel and Gretel. I mean, like, remember the witch type who kept grinding kids' bones to make her bread? In fact that's who the new lunchroom super even looks like. The H-and-G bonegrinder, know what I mean?"

The diversion worked. Park's father looked as if he was trying not to laugh, which made his mother give his father a look. Quickly Park smeared the food around on his plate so it would look as if he'd eaten some.

He looked up to find his sister glaring at him. "You are *soo* childish," she snapped.

"So what'd'ja grind to make this?" Park retorted.

"Eat garbage and die," Susie said.

"Had any good gingerbread houses lately, Suse?

44

Ummm. That would be good. Aren't you hungry for *real* food?''

"A gingerbread house isn't real food, dimbulb. And I've outgrown believing in witches who cook children for dinner. Although, if you ask me, someone should have fried you at birth.''

"Stop, both of you,'' Park's mother said. "Let's eat our dinner in peace. And *quiet*.''

"Great. I'm being poisoned and they expect me to die quietly,'' muttered Park. Then he stopped. He frowned.

"Park,'' his mother said warningly.

"Right,'' said Park, staring down at his plate. Hansel and Gretel. Grinding bones. Ms. Stoker.

The things all fit together somehow. But how? How?

Without realizing it, he took a bite of yogurt Stroganoff and ate it.

He looked up to see three pairs of eyes focused on him.

"What? What'd I do now? I didn't do it! Whatever it was, Susie did it.''

His mother suddenly smiled. "Never mind, dear.''

Park pushed his plate away. "May I be excused now?''

"We have blueberry pie for dessert,'' his father said, looking surprised.

But Park shook his head. "No, thanks,'' he said.

"Go ahead, then,'' said his mother.

Park stood up and took his plate into the kitchen. He scraped the leftovers into the compost bucket under the sink and put the plate in the dishwasher. Normally he would have been interested to see what was growing in the compost bucket.

But not tonight. Tonight he had a feeling that something was very, very wrong. He didn't know what it was. But it had something to do with Ms. Stoker and school.

What was it?

A sudden chill raised goose bumps on his arms.

What was going on?

He didn't know. But whatever it was, he'd suddenly lost his appetite.

CHAPTER
6

Bending over his plate, Park poked an unidentifiable object with his fork.

It didn't move.

But then, what did I expect? thought Park.

Just to be safe, he poked it again.

The whole table moved, and Park jumped back with a strangled shriek.

"Just what do you think you are doing?" Stacey's voice was angry. Looking up, Park saw Stacey and Maria standing in front of him. Stacey had slammed one hand flat on the lunchroom table where Park was sitting. Both girls were holding plain brown paper bags.

"Uh," began Park. "Brought your lunch, did you?"

"*We* did," said Stacey ominously.

Clutching her lunch against her body as if to shield the bag from sight, Maria sat down across from Park. "You were supposed to bring your lunch today too. In fact it was your idea!"

Stacey took the seat next to Park's and leaned close to him. Too close. Dangerously close.

If I don't do something fast, Park realized, *she's going to kill me.* But what could he do? Explain that he had a bad feeling about the new lunchroom superintendent?

"Hey, you won't believe this," he said quickly.

Stacey kept on glaring. "Try me."

"Is that health food in your lunch bag?" Jaws asked Maria sympathetically.

Maria turned toward Jaws, momentarily diverted, and Park lowered his voice. "It's an emergency. I'll explain later. Trust me!"

"Why should I trust you?" Stacey hissed. *"Traitor."*

Stacey glared at Park. Park stared back, trying to look honest, trustworthy, and true.

At last Stacey nodded. She tossed her head so her braid flipped back over her shoulder. "Okay. But it'd better be good."

"Park?" Maria said.

"I was late, Maria," said Park. "I didn't have time to fix my lunch. Honest."

"I fixed mine last night!" said Maria, outraged. "You wouldn't believe what I had to go through!"

"Hey! Great idea! Excellent idea. That's just what I'll do tonight. I'll make my lunch tonight for tomorrow. I promise."

"You'd better," Maria threatened. She looked around, then down at the wedge of pink and green on Park's tray. "What is that, anyway?"

"Mystery Casserole," said Park. "Whatever that means." He couldn't explain what had made him buy lunch. He only knew that he had to.

Maria stared down at Park's lunch tray a little longer, then opened her bag. "Maybe I'm not so mad at you after all," she said. "At least my lunch is a normal color."

Park didn't answer. The answer was going to come to him. He knew it would. It had to. He poked his food again.

Something glittered at the end of his fork. Something was looking back at him.

This time Park didn't jump. Because suddenly he knew the answer. Somehow he'd been expecting it. Somehow he'd known.

What he was looking at just pulled all the unmatched pieces of the puzzle together: Ms. Stoker. The witch in Hansel and Gretel who used to grind children's bones to make her bread.

Only it wasn't children Ms. Stoker was using in her special recipes.

"Hey!" cried Jaws, "Am I glad you didn't bring your lunch, Park. Lemme have a bite."

Before Park could stop him, Jaws had taken a spoon and scooped a big bite of the Mystery Casserole into his mouth.

"Jaws!" shouted Park.

"Jusabite," said Jaws with his mouth full. "Isgreat."

Park swallowed hard. He looked away. *I was imagining it,* he told himself. But he knew it wasn't true. He was pretty sure, almost dead certain, that he'd seen a tiny eye looking back up at him from the Mystery Casserole.

Stacey grabbed Park with one hand and savagely crumpled up her empty lunch bag with the other.

"Ouch! Hey. That hurts!" Park complained, pulling free. "What are you doing, hulking out on me?"

Without taking her eyes off Park, Stacey slam-dunked the bag into a lunchroom garbage can. "*That's* what I'd like to do to you," she said. "I had to eat my lunch, my homemade lunch, today in the middle of the lunchroom in front of *everybody*."

"I bet lots of people at other schools bring their lunches all the time," Park said reassuringly. He hated it when Stacey lost her temper. He never knew what she was going to do.

"Talk," said Stacey. "Now." She did not sound reassured. Or reassuring.

Quickly Park said, "Well, it's not a dognapping ring after all. At least not exactly."

Stacey's eyes narrowed.

"Wait, wait." Park looked around, then pulled Stacey into a corner of the lunchroom by the door. "It started at dinner last night. You know Hansel and Gretel, Stacey. Remember them? Remember the witch?"

"Did you get hit in the head or something?" asked Stacey. "Is that what you're trying to tell me?"

"Listen. It makes sense." Park raced on, telling Stacey

everything that had happened at dinner the night before—the funny feeling, the loss of appetite.

"You're sick? You have a note from your mother?" Stacey interrupted nastily.

"Will you listen?!" Park almost shouted. "I bought my lunch today because I had a feeling. And that's when I found it. The proof that pulls everything together."

Stacey frowned.

"I found"—Park looked around and lowered his voice—"I saw an eye in my Mystery Casserole."

"Park!" shrieked Stacey. "You are so gross!"

"It's true! Listen, I was wrong. I admit it. Polly didn't disappear her mom's dog. There isn't a petnapping ring at work. It's Ms. Stoker. She's not grinding the bones of little children to make her bread," Park concluded triumphantly. "She's feeding us pet food—made out of pets!"

Stacey shrieked again, throwing up her hands. Park ducked. He thought she was about to hit him. He wasn't very wrong. Stacey grabbed the sleeve of his sweater and jerked hard. "Gross! That is the grossest, most disgusting thing I have ever heard, Parker Addams! I can't believe you'd even say something like that. And if you think I'm going to fall for it—"

"*Think about it!* Ms. Stoker gets here, the lunches go from disgusting to inedible, and animals all over town start to disappear—not just dogs, but goldfish and gerbils and snakes and, and even the first grade's ant farm."

51

"No way!"

After a fast look over his shoulder Park pulled a small plastic container from his pocket. "I'm going to prove it. I swapped most of the rest of my lunch with Jaws for one of the little plastic things of raw vegetables from his lunch. I emptied out the vegetables—and this is a sample of today's lunch. I'm going to find some way to get it analyzed."

Stacey's eyes grew round. "You're serious, aren't you?"

Park held the container under Stacey's nose just to watch her lean way back. She swallowed hard. "Is it . . . is it in there?"

"Not exactly," said Park. "Jaws got to it before I could."

This time Stacey didn't shriek. She just turned green.

"Are you gonna get sick?" asked Park. "We haven't got time for that. We need evidence. We need to question Dr. Morthouse and Mr. Lucre. We need to put Ms. Stoker under surveillance . . . so are you in or out?"

"You're crazy," said Stacey. But Park could tell she was starting to believe him.

"In or out?" he repeated.

"You," Stacey answered, "are out of your mind." She pushed his hand away and stalked out of the lunchroom.

Park shoved the container back in his pocket and watched Stacey leave. He thought he'd convinced her.

If only Jaws hadn't been so fast with his spoon. That would have convinced Stacey.

But it was no use crying about that now, he told himself. What he needed was to come up with some evidence. Fast evidence. Something he could show to Stacey right now.

The double swinging doors that led from the lunchroom into the Grove School kitchen flipped open and one of the cafeteria workers trundled out, pushing a cart full of clean trays.

Idly Park watched her unload the trays and load the dirty ones onto the cart and head back into the kitchen. He'd never seen the school kitchen. The one time he'd suggested, in second grade, that his class make a class trip through the school kitchen, he'd almost gotten sent to the principal's office.

That had hurt. He'd been serious.

It still hurt.

The kitchen. The kitchen . . .

Park narrowed his eyes. If one place could produce immediate proof that what Ms. Stoker was serving wasn't USDA certified, it was the kitchen. If he could get proof, it didn't matter if Stacey believed him. Because other people would.

Trying to act casual, Park walked back toward the kitchen. The two swinging doors that led to it had high, grimy, foggy windows. Even if he could have peered through them, he wouldn't have been able to see anything.

He eased closer. A few more steps and he'd be inside.

Something stopped him. Slowly he turned.

Standing across the cafeteria, her arms folded, her eyes glinting behind her glasses, Ms. Stoker was staring right at him.

Park made a U-turn and tried to pretend he was getting a glass of water from the Caf line. Ms. Stoker never took her eyes off him as he drank the water down and deposited the glass in the dirty-dishes tray and walked out of the lunchroom.

It gave him the creeps. The lenses of Ms. Stoker's glasses had looked exactly like magnifying glasses. He felt just like an insect she was examining.

Was she suspicious of him? Had she seen him scoop up the sample of Mystery Casserole? If she had, what would she do?

Park looked back over his shoulder. The tall, skinny form of Ms. Stoker stepped out into the hall. She turned her head to the left and to the right, looking for something. Looking for someone.

Looking for me, Park thought. He took off. He didn't stop until he got to his next class.

"Ms. Stoker?"

The lunchroom super, who'd been standing in front of the menu board with an eraser in her hand, turned.

"Ah."

"Hi. I was wondering . . . remember that meat loaf?"

"Meat Loaf Surprise. My debut at Grove School. And

rather a successful one, if I do say so myself. You know, it was an experiment. I'm a creative person. I get tired of just making the same old things over and over. You've no idea."

"Do you think you could give me the recipe?" Stacey asked.

"Out of the question," said Ms. Stoker. "A chef's secrets are her stock in trade."

"Well, what about the recipe for, for Cannibal Stew? I mean, maybe you used some secret ingredient you could ah, let me know about."

"Secret ingredient?" Ms. Stoker cocked her head. "Ah, yes. Eye of newt and toe of frog." She laughed, her lips parting in a vulture's smile.

"Wh-what?" gasped Stacey.

"*Macbeth,* my dear. Shakespeare. A great writer. You'll get to him in good time."

"You get your recipes from Shakespeare?"

"Of course. After all, Shakespeare got his ideas from other writers too. But the important thing to remember is not that you borrowed an idea but what you did with the idea. That's where creative *genius* comes in." Ms. Stoker lowered her eyes modestly.

"Shakespeare?" repeated Stacey.

Ms. Stoker smiled. It was a Dr. Morthouse–calibre smile, and Stacey stepped back involuntarily.

"Maybe we'll have Meat Loaf Surprise tomorrow," Ms. Stoker told Stacey, and turned back to the menu board to erase it clean. "Just for you! I like to keep my students happy."

Stacey staggered away without answering.

What if Park were right? What if he had guessed the truth?

CHAPTER

7

Lockers slammed distantly. Gradually the sounds grew fewer and farther between. At last they stopped altogether.

Park waited.

Now the voices of teachers could be heard outside the bathroom door. Like the students they weren't wasting any time getting out of Graveyard School.

Park waited.

Someone opened the bathroom door. Quickly Park drew up his feet so they couldn't be seen under the stall door.

The bathroom door closed, and Park heard the rumbling of something heavy being wheeled down the hall. He realized that it was Basement Bart, Mr. Bartholomew, the school caretaker.

And he'd be back—to clean the bathroom.

It was now or never.

Park went to the door of the bathroom and pushed it

cautiously open. The halls of Graveyard School were dim and silent.

"Decent," said Park, taking a breath. This was easier than he'd expected. He walked out into the hall and ran down it, keeping close to the lockers and trying not to make any noise.

But his breathing sounded loud when he ducked into a stairwell. His sneakers kept making squeaking noises on the floor.

Rumble, rumble. Thump, thump, eeeeh.

Mr. Bartholomew was coming back, heading for the boys' bathroom.

Crouched behind the stairs, Park watched Basement Bart go by. He was dressed in a green army camouflage shirt and faded overalls and enormous workboots. His gray-streaked hair was pulled into a ponytail on the nape of his neck. He was enormous and he looked even bigger marching purposefully down the shadowy hall, pushing his cleaning cart.

No one messed with Basement Bart.

People said the stories he told were all true. Park had heard some of the stories.

He didn't want to mess with Basement Bart either.

The moment Basement Bart was out of sight, Park ran as fast as he could toward the lunchroom.

Late-afternoon light poured through the lunchroom windows. The shadows of the graves on the hill beyond the window stretched down like fingers reaching toward the school.

Park tried not to look as he walked toward the swinging doors that led to the kitchen.

For a moment he hesitated outside the kitchen doors. What if Ms. Stoker were on the other side? What if she never went home?

What kind of evidence was he going to find on the other side of the door?

Park didn't like to think about it. So he pushed the door open and walked into the kitchen of Graveyard School.

The smell was disgusting: dishwater and floor cleaner and all the odors of hundreds of thousands of school lunches.

I'll never eat lunch in this school again, thought Park.

The kitchen was dark, the metal surfaces of counters and ovens and huge sinks dully reflecting the light from high, square windows. It was a room without a view.

Park looked at the enormous oven, remembering Hansel and Gretel. Definitely big enough to work in the fairy tale, he thought. He made his way past racks of serving spoons and knives. The knives were hung up neatly, in ascending order of size.

The biggest knife looked like a small saw.

Park gulped and moved quickly on. The huge, empty vats made him equally uneasy. Big enough for soups and stews made from the gigantic canned foods stored beneath the counters along the walls, big enough even for him to fit into if he crouched down.

But it wasn't evidence. Just creepy.

A faint humming caught his attention. It was coming from behind a huge metal door at one end of the kitchen. The refrigerator.

If there was evidence anywhere, it would be there.

He turned the handle and pulled the door back with all his might. It swung open slowly, like the yawn of a monster mouth. Cold air like icy breath rushed out to meet him.

The refrigerator was dark. Park found a light switch outside the door. He flipped it on and stepped inside, pulling the door almost shut behind him.

Shelves of food appeared, lining either side of the refrigerator: milk, bread, cheese, mammoth heads of cabbage and forty-pound sacks of carrots and fishbowl-size jars of mayonnaise. At the far end of the refrigerator was another door.

Park paused. Had he heard something?

Basement Bart, coming to clean the lunchroom?

No. He was imagining things.

Park pushed the other door open. Freezing air stung his face and nostrils. By the light from the refrigerator Park could see a string hanging from a light bulb.

He reached up and pulled the string.

He'd never seen so much blood in all his life.

He opened his mouth to scream, but no sound came out.

And then he heard the sound of the kitchen doors thumping open.

"Eye of newt and toe of frog," a voice sang cheerfully. "Dum, dum da dee dum . . ."

Tearing his eyes from the packages of hamburger and hot dogs and bloody cuts of meat lining the shelves of the freezer, Park reached up and switched off the overhead light and pulled the door almost shut.

He was trapped in the kitchen of Graveyard School with Gladys Stoker.

CHAPTER
8

The footsteps stopped outside the refrigerator door.

Park shivered.

"What's this?" said Ms. Stoker. "The door isn't closed properly!"

As the refrigerator door opened, Park's teeth began to chatter. He tried to make them chatter quietly.

"And the light's still on! Somebody's in trouble, somebody's in trouble," chanted Ms. Stoker in a singsong voice. "Somebody's in—"

At almost exactly the same moment the light switched off, the refrigerator door closed with a thunk, and Park sneezed.

He froze.

Had Ms. Stoker heard him?

But the refrigerator door didn't open again.

Park realized he was shaking violently. He pushed the freezer door open and closed it carefully behind him. The refrigerator didn't feel much warmer.

It was pitch-black. Edging forward, Park banged into a shelf. He grabbed the edge of it and groped his way along it until he reached the door.

The door was locked. He couldn't get it open. He was trapped in the dark in the refrigerator in the lunchroom of Graveyard School.

I will not panic, I will not panic, Park told himself.

He flung himself against the door and began to scream. He screamed and screamed.

Nothing helped. No one came.

At last, exhausted, Park, turned and pressed his back against the door. *I won't starve,* he thought. *And I can't freeze to death. What else could happen?*

I get caught. I get suspended for life. My parents kill me.

It could be worse.

Standing up in the darkness, Park began to jog in place to try to keep warm. It sort of worked, but he felt stupid. No wonder his parents hated jogging.

He was bounding up and down so hard that he didn't even hear the door handle turn. He had his back to the door when it opened, framing him in the dim light of the kitchen.

"What're you doin'?" asked a rusty voice.

Park froze in mid-step.

He was rescued. He was free.

He'd been caught in the refrigerator by Basement Bart.

A hand went out and clamped down on his shoulder. With a strangled cry Park ducked, pivoted, and lurched out from under Bart's hand. He felt his shirt tear as he peeled away.

"Hey! Hey, kid!"

Park didn't answer and he didn't look back. Running at top speed, he burst through the kitchen doors, through the lunchroom doors, and into the hall. He veered down the hall toward the side entrance.

Locked.

A gravelly, menacing voice echoed down the halls. "Forget it, kid. Doors are all locked."

Park turned. Basement Bart was headed his way.

With a gasp Park ducked into a classroom.

"You can run, but you can't hide, kid." Bart's voice was much closer now. Too close.

Gasping, Park looked wildly around. He lunged toward the windows. He fumbled with the latch.

The door of the classroom opened.

"Kid," said Basement Bart. "You don't think you can get away, do you?"

Park scrabbled at the window. Pried the latch open. As he raised the window, he heard Bart right behind him.

"Gotcha," said Bart, and grabbed Park's leg.

"AAAAAAAH," screamed Park, and pitched forward through the window, kicking hard against Bart's hand.

He was free. He dropped heavily to his hands and knees, scrambled up, and sprinted away from Graveyard School as fast as he could go.

Behind him Basement Bart began to laugh.

• • •

"Park, what're you doing here? It's almost dinnertime. And you look awful!"

"Thanks," said Park, still trying to catch his breath.

"You're welcome," said Stacey.

She stood at the back door, watching Park pant for a while. Then she said, "Oh, okay. Come on in."

Park shook his head. "No. I, ah, just stopped on my way home." He'd thought he was going to tell Stacey what had happened, but what did he have to tell her? He still didn't have any evidence. He felt stupid, standing there. "Ah . . . is Morris okay?"

"He's asleep in his favorite chair," said Stacey, giving him a puzzled look.

Park nodded. He was beginning to get his breath back. He waited for Stacey to make a sarcastic remark about his pets-for-lunch theory, but she didn't. Instead she said, "Wait a minute, okay?"

Stacey disappeared into her house and returned a few minutes later holding a fat book.

"I went to the grocery store with my dad today."

"My day was more exciting," Park said.

Stacey rolled her eyes. "Anyway, there were signs all over: missing dogs, missing cats, a newt collection, a pet frog, a missing anaconda. There was a picture of the anaconda."

"Yeah? No bats?"

"It's a snake. An anaconda is," Stacey told him, frowning. "Someone even had a warning sign posted about a missing tarantula."

"Great," said Park, trying not to gag at the thought.

Stacey didn't look much happier. "I also kind of had a talk with Ms. Stoker."

"You did?" Park straightened up. Suddenly he didn't feel quite so bad.

"Yeah." Stacey made a face. "She kept going on and on, saying something about 'Eye of newt and toe of frog—' "

"You're *kidding*!"

"—and she said it was from Shakespeare, so I looked it up in my mom's Shakespeare book." Stacey opened the book and showed it to Park.

Following the direction of Stacey's finger, Park read, " 'Eye of newt and toe of frog, wool of bat and tongue of dog.' " Other phrases leaped out at him: "fenny snake" and "lizard leg."

Park reeled backward. "I don't believe it!"

"I do," said Stacey, closing the book. "About what you said. Something awful is going on at Graveyard School."

CHAPTER

9

"Polly," said Park. "When did you last see Sweetie Pie?"

Polly waved her hand breathlessly at Park and continued up the front steps of the school.

"This is very odd," murmured Maria. "The first bell should have rung."

The entire student body of Graveyard School was standing on the front steps waiting for the doors to open. The sixth-graders were gathered at the top of the stairs as usual. Park had decided to take the opportunity to try to get more evidence—by just asking questions—after his practically near-death experience with Basement Bart the day before.

Polly turned her head toward Maria and then looked wildly around. Her mouth opened, then closed.

"Polly," said Park. "Listen. Did you see anyone suspicious in the vicinity when your dog, I mean, when your mother's dog disappeared? Someone tall and thin, say, but wearing a disguise. So maybe you couldn't tell she was a woman?"

At last Polly spoke. But it wasn't to answer Park's question. "Jaws has disappeared!" she cried dramatically.

"*What?*" said Park. "No way."

Stacey felt the hairs on her neck stand up.

"It's true," said Polly. "He was waiting for the school bus this morning on the corner of his street and he forgot his gloves and his mom ran out to give them to him and"—Polly paused and took a deep breath—"he was gone."

Maria looked disgusted. "The bus came."

"Nope. I mean, the bus came, but Jaws never got on it. And guess what? *His lunch was still there*. Right there on the bench. Jaws would never go off and leave his lunch. That's what his mom says."

"That shows what a great detective you are, Polly," Park said. "Jaws hates that health food junk. He probably opened his lunch bag, saw what was inside, and broke down completely. He ran away from his lunch!"

But Polly was unshaken. "They've called everybody. Even the police!"

A moment's silence followed.

Then Polly clasped her hands together. "My mom says we're becoming crime-ridden. She says if the police had taken her report of Sweetie Pie's dognapping seriously, this wouldn't have happened now. She says—"

But neither Park nor Stacey would ever know what Polly's mother said. Because just at that moment Stacey looked at Park. Park looked at Stacey. And they both knew they were thinking the same thing.

Dognapping.

Jaws-napping.

Ms. Stoker.

Ms. Stoker had kidnapped Jaws.

Would the name of the next meal on the menu be "Jaws Soup"?

School started a little late that day. But of course none of the teachers mentioned Jaws's disappearance.

None of the kids talked about anything else.

And during his study period Park did something he'd never done before in his whole life. He asked for a pass to the principal's office.

"You want to see Dr. Morthouse?" Mr. Kinderbane, the office manager for the school, leaned over and fixed Park with steely gimlet eyes.

"Yes," said Park. His voice came out in a squeak. Clearing his throat, he repeated, more firmly, "Yes."

Mr. Kinderbane studied Park for a moment, then said, "Very well. Sit there." He pointed to an uncomfortable orange plastic chair by the door.

Park sat. He waited. He read the instructions for the Heimlich maneuver on the wall. He counted the leaves on the dusty rubber plant in the corner. He was just about to start reading the instructions for evacuation during a fire drill when Mr. Kinderbane reemerged from Dr. Morthouse's office.

"Dr. Morthouse will see you now," he said, pointing toward the door. "She's very busy. Make it succinct."

I'd like to make you extinct, thought Park.

Taking a deep breath, he walked into Dr. Morthouse's office.

No matter how many times he'd been called to the principal's office, he just couldn't get used to it—the way Dr. Morthouse loomed behind the vast desk, the way the light came through the blinds in prison-bar stripes, the way the door always closed with an awful, final thunk behind him as he walked into the room.

And this time he was doing it voluntarily.

"Uh, hi, Dr. Morthouse," said Park.

Dr. Morthouse rose from her chair to tower above Park. She didn't offer to let him sit down.

"To what do I owe the pleasure of this visit, Parker?" she asked.

"Uh, well . . . " began Park.

"Go on, you can talk to me," said Dr. Morthouse. "Trust me."

What is this, thought Park. Dr. Morthouse sounded as if she'd been taken over by Hannibal Lucre.

Dr. Morthouse said, "You and Alexander were, er, are good friends, aren't you?"

Then Park understood Dr. Morthouse's uncharacteristic oozy friendliness. *Good grief!* thought Park. *She thinks I know something about Jaws!*

Quickly he said aloud, "It's about the school lunches."

For a moment Dr. Morthouse's iron features showed a faint trace of surprise. "The school lunches?"

"Uh, yeah. I was just wondering. About Ms. Stoker, you know. Like where she went to cooking school and where she came from and . . . all that." *Great technique,* thought Parker. *I make a great detective.* But then how many detectives had to face Dr. Morthouse?

Dr. Morthouse stared at Park in disbelief. Then she said, "Ms. Stoker studied at the Rue Paris Cooking School. Her specialty, in which she did her graduate thesis recipe, was Meat Dishes. She comes to us very highly recommended. Why do you ask?"

Edging toward the door, Park groped behind his back for the doorknob and began to slide out. "No reason. Just curious . . . and she had, ah, recommendations?"

"Certainly!"

"Oh. Well, I was just curious. You know, I like learning new things and I, ah . . . " he said.

Dr. Morthouse continued to stare as Park made his escape. She was still staring as he closed the door behind him.

"Thanks," Park told Mr. Kinderbane.

Mr. Kinderbane raised a disapproving eyebrow.

Mr. Lucre was no more useful.

"A wonderful woman. A wonderful cook!" he proclaimed, rubbing his plump hands together.

Stacey stifled a sigh.

"But, like, did she come to Graveyard—er, Grove School with recommendations?"

"Certainly. The very highest," Mr. Lucre told her. He turned in the direction of the lunchroom like a weathervane and sniffed the air. "Ahhh. A new tasty treat in store for us today, I perceive."

Stacey sniffed too. Once. She decided it was best not to inhale again too deeply.

"But did you follow up on the recommendations. I mean, did you check them out?"

"Could we talk more about this later, Stacey? I think I see Ms. Stoker up ahead."

"But Mr. Lucre!"

"I just want to catch her and confirm our dinner tonight. At Maison de Cuisine." Mr. Lucre stopped suddenly and his cheeks reddened. "A business dinner of course."

He laughed. "Where do you take a chef for dinner, after all? An interesting question."

Still rubbing his hands, Mr. Lucre hurried away.

"What're we going to do?" Stacey and Park had taken refuge from lunch on the back steps of the school to compare notes from their encounters with the principal and the assistant principal.

Park folded his arms and considered Stacey's question. "I don't know. But things don't look good for Jaws. I mean, he could be the next new lunch recipe."

"Cannibal Stew," Stacey muttered. "Did you get the Mystery Casserole sample analyzed yet?"

"No," said Park. He didn't bother to explain that he didn't know where to go to get it analyzed. Or that he couldn't figure out how to explain why he wanted an analysis done.

"We've got to do *something*!" Stacey cried. "We can't just wait to see what happens."

"Why are you bringing your lunches?" demanded a voice above them.

Stacey clutched Park's arm. Park jumped a mile off the steps. "Aaack!" he cried.

"Ms. Stoker!" gasped Stacey, recovering her wits.

"Why are you bringing your lunches?" repeated Ms. Stoker, poking Stacey's lunch bag with the sharp toe of her ankle boots.

"Uh, we had leftovers and my mom wanted to make sure they got used up," said Stacey.

Ms. Stoker looked at Park.

"Me too," said Park. "I mean, leftovers."

Stacey groaned inwardly. Park was such a *feeble* liar.

Ms. Stoker seemed to think so too. She glared at Park, then at Stacey. Then almost at once she switched off her frown, replacing it with a huge and frightening smile. "Waste not, want not!" she exclaimed, raising her finger. "As I learned in my beloved alma mater. You would know what my alma mater is, wouldn't you, Parker?"

"What do you mean?" asked Parker weakly.

"My alma mater. Where I went to school. Didn't you ask Dr. Morthouse about it just this morning? All about me?"

"Not exactly," said Park.

"Ah. A misunderstanding perhaps." Ms. Stoker paused.

Neither Park nor Stacey could think of anything to say. Still smiling her frightening smile, Ms. Stoker went on, "I'm so glad we had a chance to talk, then. To clear up our misunderstandings. Perhaps we will talk more. Later."

She turned and walked away.

Stacey let go of Park's arm. Park rubbed it absentmindedly, forgetting even to complain.

"She knows," said Stacey flatly. "She knows we know. We're dead meat."

CHAPTER
10

Park winced. "Did you have to say that . . . ?" His voice trailed off. Then he socked Stacey's shoulder.

"Hey!" Stacey complained.

"I've got it! I've got it!" said Park.

"You're going to get it if you don't stop socking me," warned Stacey.

Park ignored her. "Stoker and Lucre are having dinner tonight at Maison de Cuisine, right?"

"Right," said Stacey.

"So we stake out the place. And we follow Stoker home!"

"Park, puh-lease. In the first place I bet Ms. Stoker doesn't even have Jaws at her house. And in the second place, if we want to know where she lives, we just look in the phone book."

"Oh." That stopped Park, but only for a moment. "Well, we should take a look around her house anyway. Let's go find a phone book."

But when they did find the phone book, they didn't find Ms. Stoker's name and address.

"It's probably a new listing," said Park. He fished in his pocket for change, then called information.

"I'm sorry," the operator intoned, "that is an unlisted number."

Hanging up, Park turned to Stacey. "Unlisted! That proves it!"

"All it proves is we don't know where she lives."

"Stacey!"

"Okay, okay. We'll stake out the restaurant. But I think it's useless."

"Wait till we rescue Jaws and capture Stoker! We'll be heroes."

"Or under arrest," said Stacey.

Park yawned hugely. "Gosh, I'm sleepy!"

His mother looked up from the book she was reading. "Have you finished your homework?"

"Yep. I think I'll, ah, go to bed."

"Fine, dear," his mother said, looking back down at her book.

" 'Night, son," said his father, giving Park a fatherly slug on the shoulder as Park walked by the table where he was working.

Park's sister didn't say anything. She was up in her room with the door locked.

Resisting the temptation to jiggle the door handle of his sister's room as he walked by her door, just to hear her scream in rage, Park went into his room and closed the door behind him. He took off his sweater and put on a heavy, navy-blue sweatshirt. He stuck his flashlight in the pocket of the sweatshirt and made sure he had his pocket knife. Then he made a figure out of pillows on his bed and pulled the covers up over it. He turned off his bedroom light quietly and slid his bedroom window open. Climbing out the window, he dropped into the flowerbed. He closed the window again and set off across the yard, being careful to keep to the shadows.

He stopped for a moment outside the den to look inside. His mother was still reading. His father was still working. In a little while they would go to bed.

With any luck at all he'd be back before they ever noticed he was missing.

Unless of course I get eaten first, thought Park.

In a house on a nearby street Stacey gave the pillow dummy beneath the covers on her bed a final poke. After unsuccessfully calling Information for Gladys Stoker's address, they'd called the restaurant and confirmed the reservations: eight o'clock, Mr. Hannibal Lucre and guest.

It was nearly eight o'clock. She had to hustle. She opened the door of her room and hung the PLEASE DO NOT DISTURB sign she'd swiped from the hotel on a class trip on the doorknob, stepped out into the hall, and closed the door behind her. Stooping, she unplugged the flashlight charging in the hall socket and crammed it into her pocket.

No one heard her steal down the hall to the kitchen. No one heard the ominous creak of the hinges as she opened the back door. She waited silently for what seemed like an eternity, just to make sure.

Then she zipped the dark windbreaker over her black turtleneck and slipped out the door into the night.

At first, when she got to the restaurant, she thought no one was there.

No one except the people who were eating there of course. Stationing herself behind a hedge to one side of the building, she peered out, watching

Nothing.

Then Park materialized beside her.

"I hope they weren't early," he fretted.

"Chill," said Stacey. "Look."

The two ducked back as a car swung past them into the parking lot—a big, black car that looked almost like a hearse. Right behind it was Mr. Lucre's battered old Chevy.

A moment later Ms. Stoker emerged from the hearse and waved at Mr. Lucre, who was getting out of his own car.

"Perfect timing!" she called.

"I wish you'd let me pick you up," said Mr. Lucre, slamming the door to his car and hurrying over.

"You'd never have found it," said Ms. Stoker, somewhat shortly. "Trust me." Then her voice got bright and cheerful again as she slipped her hand through Mr. Lucre's arm. "I'm looking forward to this. I've found our professional relationship so satisfying."

"I hope you find dinner just as satisfying." Mr. Lucre tittered.

"We work so hard every day for those children, don't we?" murmured Ms. Stoker.

"Gag me," said Park, watching from behind the hedge next to Stacey as the couple walked past. Ms. Stoker towered over Mr. Lucre, but he was as wide as she was tall.

"I want to ask your advice about so much. There's much I need to learn," Ms. Stoker was saying. You know, about the students, how the school really works . . ."

"You can repose full confidence in me," said Mr. Lucre.

"Gag me," muttered Stacey out of the corner of her mouth.

"For example, those two children—Parker and Stacey—"

"Children!" Park was outraged.

"Be quiet!" said Stacey.

"Ah, yes. You know, young Stacey was asking me about you just today."

"Really," purred Ms. Stoker in a tone that made Stacey's blood freeze. The two went up the front steps. "Tell me more."

Stacey didn't hear the answer. The door of the restaurant opened, and the happy couple disappeared.

"She's going to get us," said Stacey, "if we don't get her first."

"C'mon," said Park.

The two slipped out of the bushes and across the parking lot. Cautiously Stacey tried the handle of Ms. Stoker's hearse.

The door was unlocked.

"I'm not gonna like this," she said, looking down at the floor of the backseat.

Park crawled in the backseat and sniffed. "Phew. This place stinks." He leaned over and looked out into the long body of the hearse. "Look. A blanket."

Pulling the blanket out of the backseat, Park sat down on the floor of the backseat. "Come on," he told Stacey.

"Now? It's going to take them hours to eat!" said Stacey.

"We can't take any chances," said Park.

Stacey groaned. Then she climbed in the backseat and closed the door behind her. She grabbed one end of the blanket and lay down on the floor of the car and pulled it over up to her shoulders.

A flash of lightning lit the night and then, far away, a rumble of thunder.

"Great, just great," said Stacey, and settled in for a long, long wait.

CHAPTER
11

"What a lovely evening!" said a familiar gravelly voice above their heads.

Stacey jerked the blanket up over her head and pressed her face against the floor of the car.

Another flash of lightning lit up the sky—and the lumpy outline of two figures hiding beneath an old blanket on the floor of the backseat of Ms. Stoker's big, black, hearselike car parked in the parking lot of Maison de Cuisine.

"I'm honored to have you share my umbrella with me," said Mr. Lucre.

The strange, oddly familiar gravelly sound, Stacey realized, was Gladys Stoker, not laughing but giggling. The sound gave Stacey a chill even colder than the wind that was moaning in the trees.

"Why, Mr. Lucre, not a drop of rain is falling," Ms. Stoker said.

A moment's silence followed.

"Grossss," hissed Park. "I can't believe they're doing that."

"Keep your head down!" Stacey ordered out of the side of her mouth.

"Why? They're busy sucking face."

"Shut *up,* Park."

The silence was broken by Gladys Stoker laughing again, punctuated by a shrill machine-gun staccato.

Mr. Lucre was joining in the merriment.

Another short silence followed. Then the door of the car opened and Ms. Stoker got inside. Stacey and Park heard the jingle of keys, the slam of the door.

"We must do this again soon," said Mr. Lucre. "Gladys," he added boldly.

"I'd like that very much, Hannibal," purred Ms. Stoker. She started the car, and a few minutes later the hearse and its passengers was pulling out the parking lot.

For a little while Stacey tried to keep count of stops and turns. But it became too confusing. She hoped Park was having better luck.

In the front seat Ms. Stoker began to hum. Then she popped a tape in her sound system. The blast of music made Stacey jump. Park's elbow shot out and connected with her ribs warningly.

"Ah," murmured Ms. Stoker. "The sound track from *Sweeney Todd.* Now, there's music!"

The ride seemed to go on forever. Stacey's nose began to itch. She thought longingly of scratching it. Or sneezing. Or both. She raised the edge of the blanket to get some air.

Another turn. Then the car began to bounce up and down. Ms. Stoker turned the music up. Stacey shifted her weight slightly and accidentally kicked Park. She heard him give a muffled grunt.

Fortunately Ms. Stoker was now singing with the music. They bounced along at a body-bruising pace, seeming to drive only in potholes and ruts, until at last the car began to slow down.

The coat Ms. Stoker had flung over the seat started to slide slowly off it—and onto the floor of the backseat.

Stacey froze in horror.

Then Park's hand shot up and caught the coat before it was completely off the seat.

The car stopped.

Keys jingled. The door opened. Ms. Stoker's hand came out and reached toward the coat.

And Park's hand.

This time Stacey gave Park the elbow. Involuntarily he let go of the coat.

Just as Ms. Stoker's hand closed around it.

Humming a gravelly tune, she pulled the coat over the seat and got out of the car, slamming the door behind her.

The two lay for a long time on the floor of the car, not daring to move. At last Park raised his head.

"We're heeeere," he said in a soft, eerie tone.

Cautiously Stacey sat up and peered over the seat. Ahead, through the front window, she could see the dim outline of a huge old house. A sudden flash of lightning lit up the scene, revealing a sagging porch, splintering stairs, windows framed by lopsided shutters. No welcoming light shone above the front door. No lights from other houses pierced the gloom nearby.

In the roll of thunder that followed, Stacey realized that there *were* no other houses.

"Where are we?" muttered Park.

"I don't know," whispered Stacey. "But wherever it is, it's in the middle of *nowhere*."

"Makes sense," said Park. "She doesn't want any witnesses. Okay. Let's go."

Neither of them moved.

"Let's go," Park repeated.

"Okay," said Stacey.

Lightning flashed overhead. In the jagged light Stacey's eyes met Park's.

"Good grief," said Park. He reached over and carefully opened the door and slid out of the car and crouched in the shadows. A moment later Stacey slid out to join him, pushing the car door closed but not quite shut.

"Let's check it out," said Park. "I'll go around one side of the house and you go around the other. We'll meet back here in five minutes."

"Park, are you crazy? This is what happens in horror movies. The people split up and then the maniac kills them off, one by one."

"Ms. Stoker's in the house," Park pointed out.

"I don't like it," said Stacey.

"Five minutes," Park said, fading into the darkness.

Grimly Stacey crouched down and raced to the edge of the porch. Keeping low, she worked her way around the side of the house, using the gnarled, overgrown shrubbery that was twisting and whipping in the increasing gusts of wind as cover. Shadows danced macabrely along the ground, and each flash of lightning made her jump.

But not as much as the light that suddenly flashed on above her, pinning her in its beam.

Instinctively Stacey leaped back. She stumbled over something hard and fell to the ground with a thump.

The beam of light didn't follow her.

Stacey realized that someone had turned the light on in a room inside the house. She inched away from the square of light that shone on the ground below the window, then stood up and edged her way to the window. Standing on tiptoe, she peered into the room.

It was the kitchen. Ms. Stoker, wrapped in a huge white apron that looked like a choir robe, was bending over an enormous pot on the stove. In one hand she was holding a slotted spoon. With the other she was turning up the blue flame beneath the pot.

Lying on the kitchen table was a key ring with an ornate, old-fashioned key attached.

And next to that the most enormous butcher knife that Stacey had ever seen.

CHAPTER

12

"Jaws!" gasped Stacey. At the stove Ms. Stoker stopped stirring and turned. Stacey froze with horror. Ms. Stoker had heard her!

But Ms. Stoker didn't look toward the window. Instead she looked down at the table, then across the room—at a red wooden door with a huge old lock on it.

A smile that chilled Stacey to the bone crossed Ms. Stoker's face.

Turning back around, Ms. Stoker took a large plate out of the pantry and ladled what looked like Cannibal Stew onto it. Still smiling, she crossed the room, picked up the key, and opened the door.

A light shone from below.

It was the door to the basement.

"Your favorite," sang Ms. Stoker. She disappeared down the basement stairs.

Stacey leaped back from the window and, turning, began to run around the side of the house with all her might.

As she crossed the overgrown front lawn, the lightning flashed and the thunder rumbled loudly.

And someone grabbed her from behind.

Stacey gave a stifled cry and swung wildly. Her knuckles connected with something hard.

"OW!"

"OW!"

"Park!"

"Who'd you expect? C'mon!" Park grabbed Stacey's elbow and began to drag her with him.

"Park, Park," panted Stacey. "Ms. Stoker was cooking Cannibal Stew. And that's Jaws's favorite, remember? I think she's got him in the basement."

"I know," said Park.

"You *know*. How do you know?"

"I saw him." They rounded the side of the house. Abruptly Park crouched even lower and pulled Stacey into the bushes.

A faint glimmering of light shone at their feet.

Park held his finger to his lips warningly, then knelt by the glimmer of light. He pointed.

Kneeling beside Park in the shrubbery that surrounded the house, Stacey looked in the direction that Park was pointing. It was a window. A tiny, filthy wire-mesh window half-covered with the dirt of the flowerbed.

Park and Stacey bent forward to look through the window.

They were looking down into the basement of Ms. Stoker's house.

Cages and terrariums and shelves lined one wall. Most of them were empty, but a few of the cages had dogs and cats inside. A complete home-entertainment center lined the other.

"Wow," whispered Stacey. "Look at that sound system . . ."

"Stacey," said Park.

Stacey jerked her attention away from the home-entertainment center and leaned closer to the window.

In the middle of the room was a table and chair. Sitting at the table, holding a spoon in one hand and the remote control of the monster color television across the room in the other, was Jaws. Standing by him, smiling, Ms. Stoker was watching him eat.

So were the cats and dogs in the cages.

"This is great," they heard Jaws say. He patted his stomach. "My pants fit again."

"I know," said Ms. Stoker.

"What's for dessert?" Jaws said.

"Clean your plate and you'll see," Ms. Stoker promised.

"No problem," said Jaws.

Ms. Stoker smiled.

Both Stacey and Park recoiled involuntarily.

But Jaws never noticed the predatory flash of Ms. Stoker's teeth. He pointed the remote and clicked, channel surfing intently as he wolfed down his Cannibal Stew. He didn't even notice that Ms. Stoker had left the basement.

"We've got to go for help," said Park. "Boy, when

91

everyone sees this setup, Ms. Stoker is going to be in big trouble!''

"Park, we *can't* go for help," said Stacey. "We don't know where we are. And it would take too long."

"I'm not going in there alone," said Park. "Did you see that smile?"

"You should see the knife she has on the kitchen table upstairs," said Stacey.

Park shook his head. "Jaws'll never fit through this window."

"Maybe one of us could create a distraction, and then you could sneak in the house and go down in the basement and get Jaws," said Stacey.

"Me?" said Park.

Below, Jaws finished his plate of stew. He pushed himself back from the table and rubbed his stomach.

Lightning flashed and the wind began to moan more steadily in the trees.

"Park, look!" Stacey pointed.

"What?"

Stacey pulled her flashlight from her pocket and flicked it on for a brief moment. Just down from them was a dark shape in the middle of the shrubbery.

"A door?" said Park.

"An old storm door to the cellar. Remember? Like the one they went down through in *The Wizard of Oz*? Before the tornado?"

Park was silent for a moment. Then he said, "Yeah.

And I bet Jaws would fit through *that*. But how do we get it open?"

"Ms. Stoker? I'm finished. Can I have seconds?" called Jaws.

"*May* I have seconds?" Ms. Stoker's muffled voice corrected Jaws from above. Jaws rolled his eyes.

"May I?"

"Certainly," answered Ms. Stoker. "Just a minute."

Jaws leaned back to wait.

"And I have a surprise for you!" added Ms. Stoker.

Jaws raised the remote control and turned the volume up to high. Jaws smiled. "Cool!" he shouted over the noise.

"A surprise!" gasped Stacey. "Did you hear that? We're running out of time!"

Stacey lunged for the storm door, dragging Park with her.

"I can't see," complained Park. Stacey bent closer, keeping her hand cupped around the flashlight so that only the thinnest beam touched on the storm door.

"This is the mother of all padlocks," Stacey muttered.

Park grunted. He slid one hand under the padlock and lifted it up, giving it an experimental yank. The rusty sound of metal on metal made Stacey's fillings ache.

They both froze.

But the only sound they heard was the moaning of the wind through the trees and the now-distant rumble of thunder. In one part of her mind Stacey noted that the storm seemed to be passing them by after all.

Park gave the lock another yank. The sound was even worse the second time.

"It's locked," he said, squatting back on his heels.

"Duh," said Stacey. She leaned forward and examined the lock. Rust had eaten parts of it away.

But not enough for it to break.

"We're never going to make it in time," said Park. "We should break the window and warn Jaws. Maybe he could—"

"It's wood," said Stacey.

"So? You planning on setting it on fire . . . ?" Park's voice trailed off as he considered the possibility.

"Not a bad idea," Stacey said. "But I bet it'd be a lot easier just to undo the hinges on one side."

She turned the thin beam of the flashlight toward the hinges. They were old and rusted to the max too. But they were just hinges.

"Cool," said Park. He reached in his pocket and pulled out his Swiss Army knife. "Fortunately a detective is always prepared."

Stacey reached in her pocket and felt the reassuring outline of her own Swiss Army knife. "Right."

"We've got to hurry!" Park bent down and opened the knife to the screwdriver attachment and set to work unscrewing the hinges on one side. Stacey went to work on the other. It was slow going in the unsteady beams of the flashlights. And Stacey kept thinking she heard sounds. The soft sounds of footsteps. The rustling of skirts. But it was hard to tell, especially since the loudest sound of all was the noise from Jaws's television set in the basement.

Her hands began to sweat.

"I . . . almost . . . got it. Got it!" gasped Park at last.

"I can't believe she didn't hear us," said Stacey. "There. That does it."

"Relax," Park said. "In all this wind she's not going to hear a little scraping sound. Especially with the TV on."

Together the two lifted the storm door free. In the faint light from the bottom of the basement they could see steep, narrow, slimy stairs festooned with cobwebs. The blast of sound from the television leaped up the stairs toward them.

"Ladies first," said Park promptly.

"Jerks last," answered Stacey, and leaned gingerly forward.

"AAAAAAAAH! NOW I HAVE YOU!"

Lightning flashed. Thunder rumbled. And Stacey and Park began to scream as Ms. Stoker came running down the back stairs of her house, holding her carving knife high in the air.

"Run!" screamed Park.

"Run!" screamed Stacey.

They jumped up to run and crashed into each other. Park's flashlight flew into the air and landed with an ominous crunching sound, going out.

"Split up," gasped Park. scrambling to his knees.

"Trying," Stacey gasped back.

Ms. Stoker lumbered toward them, waving the knife. "I know who you are!" she cried. "You'll never get away!"

"Arrrgh!" cried Park, dodging out of the shrubbery

and narrowly eluding the maddened lunchroom super-intendent.

Stacey wasn't so lucky. One moment she was scrambling to her hands and knees and the next minute the ground was giving way beneath her.

No. Not the ground. The edge of the stone steps leading down into Gladys Stoker's cellar.

With a bloodcurdling scream Stacey fell down the cellar stairs.

"Stacey? What are you doing here?"

Stacey opened her eyes and groaned. Jaws Bennett's round face danced above her like a weird full moon. She closed her eyes again and croaked, "Where's Park?"

"Park? Is he here too?"

It took all her willpower to open her eyes again, but she did. "Yes."

Looking around as if he expected to see Park materialize out of thin air, Jaws said, "Where?"

"Upstairs. Outside. Stacey pulled herself to a sitting position and cautiously stretched.

Painful, but not fatal, she decided.

At least not yet.

The sound of dogs barking and cats meowing brought her back to her senses. For a moment she'd forgotten. But now it was all coming back to her.

"Jaws," she said urgently. "How long have I been down here?"

Jaws blinked. "You just fell down the stairs. Out of nowhere. What's going on?"

"I haven't been unconscious long?"

"Were you unconscious?" Jaws leaned over to peer into Stacey's eyes. "Your eyes were open the whole time. But they did look kind of funny, just for a minute there."

"Okay, okay, never mind my eyes." Stacey got up and leaned to look up the basement steps. What was happening up there? All she could see was darkness. And all she could hear was the rustling of shrubbery in the wind.

"C'mon, Jaws, we gotta go!" Stacey put her foot on the bottom step.

But Jaws stopped her. "Why?" he whined. "It's late and cold. And I haven't even had dessert."

Stacey's jaw dropped. She turned and stared.

Jaws was standing in the middle of the room, his arms folded across his chest.

"Jaws! Get with the program! You've been *kid-napped*!"

"Oh. That." Jaws shrugged. "I'm going home in a few days. It's just to teach my parents a lesson. Maybe next time they'll think twice before feeding me carrots marinated in Vitamin E oil."

"You came here voluntarily?"

"Well, Ms. Stoker offered me a ride, see? And we started talking. And we figured this all out."

99

"So why are you locked in the basement?" Stacey demanded.

"Am I?" Jaws shrugged. "I never checked. I mean, I've got everything I want down here. Giant TV. Videos. Vid games. Food. As much food as I want. And I don't even have to go to school."

"Yes, you do," muttered Stacey. "As lunch."

"I'm not leaving," stated Jaws.

Stacey marched over to Jaws and grabbed his shirtfront. *"Yes, you are,"* she snarled. "Ms. Stoker has you here, fattening you up, so you can be the next secret ingredient in one of her experimental school-lunch recipes. What do you think those animals are for in the cages over there? Where do you think all the pets and things have been disappearing to around here? What do you think *used* to be in some of those empty cages."

Jaws's face turned bright red. "I don't believe you."

"Fine. But you're coming with me. Now."

"Okay, okay, but wait a minute, will ya?" Jaws reached out and grabbed a stack of video games and begin stuffing them in his pants pockets.

Stacey grabbed him and yanked him toward the stairs. She peered up into the murky dark. She'd lost her flashlight in the fall.

And she'd lost Park. Had he gotten away? Was he going for help?

Or was Ms. Stoker at that very moment . . . ?

Stacey shuddered. Keeping a firm grip on Jaws's arm, she started up the steps. Then she stopped.

100

What if it was a trap? What if Ms. Stoker was waiting at the top of the stairs with her carving knife . . . ?

"Are we going, or what?" asked Jaws peevishly.

"We're going, we're going," answered Stacey. She took a deep breath and headed up the stairs. She'd almost reached the top when she heard a sound that raised the hair on the back of her neck.

A familiar voice calling softly, "Stacey . . . Staceeeeeeee."

CHAPTER
14

"Yo, Park, is that—ow!" said Jaws. "Whatd'ja punch me for?"

"Because it could be a trap," Stacey said.

"A trap! Stacey, you'd better get up here now! Ms. Stoker is out there in the woods somewhere, but she'll be ba—"

Park's voice faded, and they heard him running away. "You'll never catch me alive!" he cried.

And from a little farther away Ms. Stoker answered, "Alive? Hahahahahaha."

"Come on! Now!" ordered Stacey. Holding tightly to Jaws's arm, she stumbled up the basement stairs and into the dark night above.

"This way," she hissed. Her groping hand hit something cold and hard and familiar. Her flashlight, half buried in the dirt and still on. Clicking it quickly off, she pocketed it gratefully, then began to make her way back around the side of the house under the cover of the over-grown shrubbery in the flowerbed.

A flash of lightning illuminated the scene as they reached the front of the house.

The hearselike car still loomed in the driveway. The skeletal trees still twisted and cracked their knuckly branches in the wind.

And Stacey still didn't know where they were.

"Do you remember the way you got here?" she asked Jaws.

Jaws said sulkily, "No. I was eating a piece of pizza."

"Great, just great." A crashing sound from the nearby bushes told her that Park or Ms. Stoker or both were nearly upon them.

"Run!" she said, and before Jaws could protest, she'd pulled him out of the bushes with her and was dragging him across the front yard.

They ran past the car. They ran through a narrow opening in the trees onto what had once been a road. Jaws stumbled, nearly pulling Stacey over.

"Slow down," he complained.

"You're right," Stacey said softly. "We'll have to go slow on this road." She didn't tell Jaws about her flashlight. She didn't want to risk being seen using it.

"Aha! I've got you now!" shrieked a gravelly voice.

"Park! Oh, no!" moaned Stacey, stopping in her tracks. Screams filled the night.

"Park!" cried Stacey.

A figure burst out of the woods near them. It stumbled, lurched, then headed straight for them.

Stacey stopped and turned to face it, prepared to use her flashlight as a weapon and fight to the death.

The figure came closer, closer.

Then Park shouted almost in Stacey's ear, "What're you waiting for! Run for your life!"

How long had they run in horrible slow motion down the twisted, rutted old road? Stacey didn't know. She'd lost count of the times she'd fallen, lost count, too, of the number of times she'd said, "Shut up, Jaws," when Jaws had started to whine.

They stumbled noisily, desperately on, until at last Park gasped, "I haven't heard anything for a while. I think we've lost her."

He bent over, his hands on his knees, trying to catch his breath.

"She wouldn't hurt us," said Jaws for about the hundredth time. But his voice didn't have as much conviction as it had at first. Neither Park nor Stacey bothered to answer him.

They were too tired.

"I still have my flashlight," Stacey managed to get out after a few minutes. "I didn't say anything before because we couldn't have used it anyway."

"What?" said Jaws indignantly.

"Good thinking," said Park, straightening. "But we can use it now."

Stacey reached in her pocket. If they stayed on this road, they'd come to another road sooner or later. And sooner or later one of those roads would lead them back to town.

To safety.

She took the flashlight out of her pocket and held it up and flicked the switch.

And the three of them were pinned in the double beam of headlights bearing down on them.

"Stoker! The car," cried Stacey. She swung the beam of the flashlight toward the woods.

The car roared toward them. It was almost on top of them. Stacey heard a familiar sound.

"Hahahahahahah!"

Ms. Stoker was laughing.

At the last possible moment Stacey and Park, pulling Jaws between them, plunged off the narrow track and into the deep, dark woods.

The car swung off the road too. It followed them into the woods, the powerful headlights silhouetting them against the trees as they tried to escape.

"Noooo!" screamed Park. "Noooooo!"

CHAPTER
15

There was a horrible grinding noise. The headlights of the car slashed up into the sky and stopped.

Stacey looked back over her shoulder. Ms. Stoker's car had crashed to a halt against a huge tree. It was tilted slightly back and over on its side. One of its front wheels spun uselessly in the air.

The three plunged sideways out of the light and into the safe darkness of the woods.

Behind them the laughter had stopped.

The lightning flashed overhead, one last bolt.

Then through the clearing in the trees, the three saw the glint of water.

"A stream," said Park.

"We can follow that," Stacey said.

"What good will that do?" complained Jaws.

"It'll keep us from going in circles," Stacey snapped. "And it's bound to lead us somewhere."

She pointed the beam of her flashlight toward the water, and in a minute they were headed downstream.

"Tooee, tooee," a bird called from a nearby pine tree, startling Stacey.

They'd walked for a long, long time without speaking. Now, looking up in the direction of the bird, Stacey realized that the dark sky overhead was turning faintly gray.

"It'll be morning soon," she volunteered.

No one answered. They kept moving, heads down, following the stream. Their feet were wet and muddy. Their clothes were torn and filled with stickers.

And Jaws was hungry.

"We're almost there," Park said a moment later.

"Almost where?" asked Jaws.

Park pointed. "Look," he said.

They'd come to a road. A real road. One that had a road sign on it with the name of their town and the words FIVE MILES.

"We may make it back by breakfast, Jaws," said Park.

"I hope so," said Jaws.

The sun was turning the east golden yellow when Stacey broke the silence nearly five miles later. "No one's going to believe us," said Stacey. "We don't have any proof."

"We saved Jaws," answered Park.

"You did not!" said Jaws. "I could've saved myself if I'd wanted to. And I don't believe you either. I had it good there, until you guys came along. You were just jealous!"

108

"You're whacked, Jaws, you know that?" Park began. Then he caught Stacey's eye.

She was making a goofy face.

A face as goofy as he felt.

Park started to laugh. So did Stacey. The two of them laughed and laughed, standing by the side of the road at the edge of town, Jaws in between them, his arms folded in annoyance.

At last Stacey straightened up and gasped. "No one's going to believe us."

"You won't get in trouble," Jaws promised kindly. "*I'll* think of something. Even though you should have minded your own business you know. But I guess you thought you were helping. . . ."

With that he turned and marched down the road in the direction of his house.

"Good grief," said Stacey indignantly.

"He'll forget it by tomorrow." Still grinning, Park rubbed his face with his hands. "I'm hungry," he said.

And he and Stacey burst into laughter all over again.

Jaws Bennett looked around the kitchen of his house. He'd let himself in with the key his parents kept under the third brick from the left on the right side of the front walk. It was too early to wake them up, he reasoned. And he was a considerate kid.

Besides, he was hungry. Once his parents were up, who knew when he'd get a decent meal? Time enough for all that in a little while. But first he was going to eat.

• • •

The back door was still unlocked when Stacey got home. She opened it as quietly as possible, checking out the time on the kitchen clock as she went through. Half an hour still before her father got up.

As quietly as she could, she slipped down the hall and into her room. Her clothes were ruined. She stuffed them into the back of her closet. She'd smuggle them out later and get rid of them.

Despite her aches and pains she managed to wash most of the grime and dirt off and get into her nightshirt just as she heard the first round of alarms go off in her parents' bedroom.

She shoved the pillows back into place on her bed and got under the covers.

And remembered that they did have proof. Park had that sample of the Mystery Casserole. That would prove them right after all.

Smiling, she closed her eyes and fell instantly asleep.

Park climbed back through his window. It was as easy as it had been climbing out.

He took off his wet, muddy shoes and after a moment's thought threw them in the laundry hamper along with the rest of his clothes.

He looked at the lumpy pillow figure sleeping peacefully in his bed. He'd be there soon.

He smiled, thinking of sleep. And remembering that they did have proof after all of Gladys Stoker's diabolical nutritional program. The sample of Mystery Casserole was still in the refrigerator in its plastic container. He hadn't been sure who to send it to for analysis, but maybe he'd just take it to the police.

But first he had to get something to eat. He was *starving*.

Quietly he headed for the kitchen and began a high-speed assembly of leftover sandwich.

But he skidded to a halt when he opened the refrigerator door and peered in.

The sample jar of Mystery Casserole was gone.

In its place was a note in his sister's spiky handwriting. "Susie was here. Yum yum. Ha ha."

Park stared for a long time at the space where the sample had been. Then he closed the refrigerator, threw away his half-made sandwich, and went to bed.

CHAPTER
16

"Attention, students. Attention!" Dr. Morthouse, principal of Grove Elementary School, raised her hands.

The noise in the auditorium got louder.

"Jaws is a real hero," said Maria. "Can you believe he was lost all that time in the woods? And just because he thought he saw one of the missing dogs and tried to follow it and catch it. I never knew Jaws was so, so—"

"So amazing," suggested Stacey. She looked toward the front of the auditorium, where Jaws was surrounded by kids. He was holding a bag of jellybeans, popping them into his mouth by the handful.

No one had talked of anything else all weekend. Jaws had been on all the local TV stations and had had his picture on the front page of the town paper.

He was famous. And more importantly he was well fed. His parents, broken down by the ordeal of losing Jaws, had agreed to let him off the health food hook. At that very moment Jaws had an entire week's worth of school-lunch money in his pocket—to spend all in one day if he liked.

Perhaps in honor of Jaws's return Dr. Morthouse was being a little more indulgent than usual. She surveyed the packed auditorium and let the noise rage on for another half a second. Then she leaned forward. "ATTENTION!"

Something silver flashed in her mouth.

Stacey's eyes met Park's. They both slid down in their seats.

Oddly enough, along with Park, many of the missing animals had begun to turn up too.

But not Polly's mother's nasty dog. It was still among the missing.

And probably would be. Permanently.

The microphone made a horrible screaming sound.

Silence fell.

"Gooood," said the principal. Her smile seemed more forced than usual.

"Now, boys and girls."

Park groaned. Stacey rolled her eyes.

"I'm sorry to give you some very bad news. Ms. Stoker has been forced, for reasons of health, to resign her post as lunchroom superintendent. I'm sure all of you will join me in unanimous regret over our losing such an excellent and thrifty cook."

The silence that met this remark was profound.

Dr. Morthouse looked at the students and frowned. Then she turned. "Mr. Lucre?"

114

The man who walked out onto the stage of the auditorium was not the man he had once been. His bow tie was crooked. His hair was no longer combed sideways over his bald spot. His suit was crumpled.

He was a broken man.

"We will all miss Gladys Stoker," he said sadly, clutching the microphone to his breast and raising his eyes. "She brought us new culinary experiences. She was a *great* chef."

"Yeah, but is she boiling in that great cooking pot on the other side," muttered Park.

"We are fortunate, however," Mr. Lucre went on even more sadly, "that our former lunchroom superintendent, Mr. Todd, has agreed to come out of retirement until we can find someone to take the job permanently. We are grateful to Mr. Todd, who resumes his duties today. But of course no one can ever replace Ms. Stoker—on our plates or in our hearts."

Head bowed, Mr. Lucre stepped back from the microphone.

Stacey and Park exchanged glances. Each knew what the other was thinking.

Who'd ever thought they'd look forward to Mr. Todd's school lunches?

"If you were Ms. Stoker, where would you go?" asked Stacey. She and Park were sitting on a bench in the park near their neighborhood, watching Morris watch squirrels.

"Far, far away," said Park. "I don't know."

"Do you think she'd keep doing what she does?" Stacey asked.

Park shrugged. "Probably. Why?"

Stacey reached in her backpack and pulled out a section of the day's paper. "My dad was reading this at breakfast today," she explained.

Park took the newspaper out of Stacey's hand. Silently he read where she was pointing.

PETS MISSING, it said.

In a town not too far from their own all kinds of animals had started to disappear. Petnapping was suspected.

Motive was unknown.

Ms. Stoker's Recipe for Mystery Meat Loaf

Ingredients:

1 pound _____ meat
    (*type of animal*)

½ cup _____ eyes
    (*type of reptile*)

½ cup _____
    (*something slimy*)

1 tablespoon _____
    (*something smelly*)

1 pinch _____ to spice
    (*something dry*)

Instructions:

Mix all ingredients together with a _____.
    (*object*)

Then bring to a boil in a _____. Stick in
    (*container*)

a _____ for 30 minutes. Take out, cool, and
    (*another container*)

serve with a side dish of _____
    (*texture*)

_____ vegetables.
    (*color*)

Enjoy!!!

Fill in the blanks and create your own
Graveyard School creepy lunch menu!

Lunch Specials Today

_____ Soup

_____ Salad

with choice of _____ or _____ Dressing

Baked _____ Lasagna

Spaghetti with _____

Pizza with choice of three toppings:

_____, _____, or _____.

Rice and _____

Dessert: _____-Flavored Pudding.

CULPEPPER ADVENTURES
Gary Paulsen

Dunc Culpepper and Amos Binder are best friends—and they always get into trouble. Follow the fast-paced mystery adventures of the sleuthing trio and get in on all the fun as they get themselves in—and out of—trouble.

☐	40598-X	**The Case of the Dirty Bird**	$3.25/$3.99 Can.
☐	40601-3	**Dunc's Doll**	$3.25/$3.99 Can.
☐	40617-X	**Culpepper's Cannon**	$3.25/$3.99 Can.
☐	40642-0	**Dunc Gets Tweaked**	$3.25/$3.99 Can.
☐	40659-5	**Dunc's Halloween**	$3.25/$3.99 Can.
☐	40678-1	**Dunc's Journey to the Center of the Earth (Nov. 92)**	$3.25/$3.99 Can.
☐	40686-2	**Dunc and the Flaming Ghost**	$3.25/$3.99 Can.
☐	40749-4	**Amos Gets Famous**	$3.25/$3.99 Can.
☐	40756-7	**Dunc and Amos Hit the Big Top**	$3.25/$3.99 Can.
☐	40762-1	**Dunc's Dump**	$3.25/$3.99 Can.
☐	40775-3	**Dunc and the Scam Artists**	$3.25/$3.99 Can.
☐	40790-7	**Dunc and Amos and the Red Tattoos**	$3.25/$3.99 Can.